My Heart Belongs in

Silver City,

Nevada

Charlotte's Misadventure

Book ♡ One

Samantha Bayarr

Newly Released books
99 cents or FREE with
Kindle Unlimited.

♡ LOVE to Read?
♡ LOVE 99 cent Books?
♡ LOVE GIVEAWAYS?

Table of Contents

Prologue

Silver City, Nevada, Summer, 1861

Rooster Figg sat across from Beau Dalton, making note of his tell. It was as subtle as biting down on the stale cigar clenched between his crooked, stained teeth that showed his age more than the deep creases that cinched his forehead. The older man clenched his cards with a tight fist, his gray, wiry brows narrowed over a set of dark eyes. The man had had too many years to season his mean spirit, and Rooster was no match for him.

Rooster could only hear the beating of his heart. It blocked out the rowdy piano and saloon entertainment that would make his ma cringe if she knew he was in the house of sin. If his pa or ma could see him now, they'd be ashamed, but he needed the pile of money in front of him. More than that, he wanted the deed to the mine Beau had put up as collateral.

His pa's watch was the only thing besides his little sister that meant anything to him in this world. His pa's solid gold pocket watch that was handed down to him from his pa before him.

He held it in his fist close to his heart, pausing before tossing it in the *kitty* along with Beau's lot.

Forgive me, Pa.

It was done; there would be no turning back now. He told himself his pa would understand. After all, it was for Charlotte. Otherwise, he'd have backed down. Before he'd left her at the Barbary Coast, Mr. Wilkins from the bank had taken their small shack, and he'd left her with his ma's friend. He'd promised to send for her as soon as he was settled, but more than three months had passed already, and he was never so close to having the means to fetch her as he was now.

There was too much at stake; he needed that deed to the mine almost as much as he needed his next breath.

To own a piece of Nevada territory was important to him, and he knew he wouldn't get it mucking out stalls and mending fence as a ranch hand at the Circle B Ranch for Beau Dalton. Normally, he wouldn't venture away from the small-stake games in the bunkhouse especially since most of the men there always seemed to have more money than he had, but he'd put it all in for this chance to win that mine.

For him, it meant freedom from the less-than scrupulous ways that Beau ran his ranch. His foreman and most of his hands were always willing to do whatever the man demanded of them whether it was legal or not. Rooster had been the exception to that. He'd teetered his last chance with Sheriff Tucker doing Beau's bidding, and if he won this hand, he'd be a free man—free to set up camp on his own little piece of the territory. He'd much rather live in a pitched tent than the bunkhouse at a ranch of ill-gotten gain, and immoral standards of operation.

But here he was, sitting in the saloon and fully ready to gamble away his last piece of family history, and his sister's future as a respectable woman. He glanced around at the painted ladies serving drinks and draping themselves over the cowhands just to get their hands on the drunken men's money.

He blinked and shook off the guilt, and said a little prayer that his hand would win—for the sake of Charlotte's virtue. His ma and pa would roll over in their graves if he caused his baby sister to live the life of a soiled dove. His job was to provide for her, and so far, he'd failed her in more ways than one.

He studied the cards in his hand, relaxing his features and trying his best to keep his tells in check. A bead of sweat rolled down the middle of his back; he swiped his Stetson from his head and fanned his face a moment and then pushed it back down again. The action distracted Beau only for a moment, but it was just long enough for him to consider one last time if he could pull this off.

There were several combinations that could beat him, but the odds were in his favor that Beau was bluffing; his clenched teeth gave him away. Rooster stared at the three ladies and the ace in his hand; he was drawing for that fourth lady or another ace to give him a full house, but when Beau slid his card across the table, he was almost two afraid to pick it up.

Don't react, he told himself as he lifted the corner to glance at it.

He knew the mine itself was worthless— Beau had said as much, but having the property meant he would be able to live on his own land. It was the only way he could be his own man. There was always a chance it would produce enough silver to keep him in salt pork and beans, and if he was lucky, a little coffee. But he was smart enough to understand that Beau would not have included it if he thought it was worth more than a plugged nickel.

He knew better than to go up against Beau, but he was just desperate enough to think he had a chance—either that, or he was just plain loco.

Another deuce. He paused; three of a kind was still a good hand, and unless Beau had been dealing from the bottom of the deck, he'd won.

Rooster laid his cards down, Beau still clenching his cards with a tight fist.

He made a pass for the kitty, but Beau drew his gun and clicked back the hammer.

Rooster froze.

"Not so fast, saddle-tramp," Beau said as he placed his hand down on the table. "My three aces beat your three ladies, which makes that money, including your daddy's pocket watch, *mine!*"

He scooped up the watch from the top of the kitty and wound it, the corners of his mouth lifting to a full smile.

Rooster's blood boiled. He swallowed a lump in his throat as he watched the man examine the watch before he put it in his vest pocket; it surprised him that such a loss could hit him so hard. He thought he'd hardened his heart to the loss of his pa after he'd left San Francisco, but now, it was as if he'd lost him all over again.

"You cheated!" Rooster said, rising from his chair and letting it scrape the wood floor.

Beau leaned forward, hugging the pile of money on the table. "I'll tell you what, saddle-tramp," he said, his cigar clenched between his teeth. "I'll give you a chance to *earn* that pocket watch back; I'll even throw in the deed to the mine, seeing as you wanted it bad enough to hock your daddy's watch for it."

Rooster sat back in his chair and tossed his hat on the chair beside him. "Let's play; winner takes all."

Beau threw his head back and laughed as he plucked his Stetson from his balding head. He leaned in and scooped his winnings into his hat and looked up at Rooster.

"I'm already the winner, and I've taken all of it, wouldn't you agree?" Beau asked. "So, the way I see it, you've only got one way to get this back—you can come back to work for me for six months at half-pay."

"I'm not working for you for free!" Rooster said, jumping up from his chair again. "I practically already do."

"You're forgetting one important detail here; you were fired the minute you sat in front of me and challenged me to a game of cards, and you're real lucky I don't shoot you for accusing me of cheating. Of course, you and I both know I'd have more fun drumming up some charges against you, so the sheriff has to arrest you, but we both know you'd be swinging from a tree long before the circuit judge made it to town to acquit you."

Rooster slipped a finger between his neck and his bandana and yanked on it, thinking it suddenly felt like he was being hanged from it. "Alright, I'll work for you—for six months, and at the end of that time, I walk away with my pa's pocket watch and the deed to the mine."

He extended his hand to Beau, but the man refused it.

"This was nothing more than a gentleman's agreement; if we shake hands, that would make it legal, and I just don't know if I can live up to that. You'll just have to trust me for it," Beau said, chuckling.

Rooster clenched his jaw, but nodded. He didn't trust Beau, but he had no other choice; everything he held dear to him depended on that agreement.

ONE

Nevada Territory, Summer, 1862

One year later…

Charlotte Figg bit her tongue—again. This time, she tasted blood.

Every time the wheels of the stagecoach sank into a deep rut along the trail without warning, she suffered the consequence of her decision to make the long journey in search of her brother.

Neither her physical pain nor her broken heart would cause her to weep in front of her traveling companion. She was just that determined to keep to herself.

"Is this your first trip away from home?" the young woman asked.

Home; I haven't had a place to call home for more than a year.

Charlotte nodded; to give any details would only invite more questions that she wasn't in the mood to answer.

A booming, mining town was no place for a proper lady to travel to unescorted, and if her pa was still alive, he'd have reprimanded her for such a foolish notion and forbidden her to go. More than a year had passed since he'd been laid to rest, and she'd grown impatient waiting for word from her brother.

Her gut warned her to search for him.

Bone-weary from the uncomfortable ride on the Wells Fargo stagecoach from Reno where she'd disembarked the train, Charlotte longed to stretch her legs and wipe away the thick layer of trail-dust caked on her skin. Blinking away the dust from her lashes, she pulled a handkerchief from her reticule and swiped at the grit that stung the corners of her eyes. She bit down, grinding the grit between her teeth.

She sighed. *If I'd wanted to dine on this forsaken land, I would have scooped up a mouthful of it and swallowed it down with a bottle of sarsaparilla.*

She shifted in her seat, wincing as her hips suffered another jolt. Unable to sit upright without it becoming a chore, she forced a half-smile to cover her frustration. She pulled at the bottom corner of her corset through the bodice of her dress and took a deep breath.

She coughed, choking down another mouthful of Nevada territory, and she could stand it no longer. She covered her mouth with the handkerchief tucked up her sleeve, and inconspicuously wiped muddy spittle from her lips disguising her unladylike manners as best as she could.

The jangling of the harnesses and the grinding of the wheels in the hard-packed dirt hammered out a rhythm in her head, causing pain to creep up along her temples. Miles of desert had passed by the cutout window in the door, a thick cloud of dust masking the plain landscape and settled on her linen, goldenrod skirt and jacket.

She chided herself for not having the forethought to wear a plain brown traveling dress.

She pushed stray auburn curls behind her ears and slapped at the folds of the fabric, frustrated by the clouds of dry earth that permeated even her bloomers, tainting them to match the layer of soil that bronzed the isolated trail. Her dry throat begged for a sip of cool well-water to wash down the trail dust, but they were a considerable distance from the nearest way-station. She'd measured the long miles in her head, ticking off each one impatiently, hoping it was the last.

The telegram announcing her arrival hadn't yielded an answer, and she counted the days until she could look into her older brother's green eyes that mirrored her own. Would this long and dirty journey ever end? He'd left her in the care and company of their ma's friend, Mrs. Billings, who owned a boarding house in San Francisco. He'd departed on the train just hours after pa's funeral, and she'd heard nary a word from him since.

What had he been thinking, leaving her alone with the old woman? She could no more take care of herself; to add Charlotte to the woman's burdens was nothing short of foolish. He should have known better, but she doubted he was any more right in his mind than she was at the time. She knew her brother too well; he had run away from his feelings, not her, but that still didn't make it right. She prayed for him daily, but it didn't quiet her annoyance with him for neglecting her the way he had.

Worry and disappointment drove her to look for him, and she was determined to find an end to this miserable trail no matter how uncomfortable it became. She had no idea if her brother worked in the mines, or if he would even greet her once she arrived. His promise to send for her after staking his claim in Silver City was long-overdue, her growing impatience and dwindling funds forced her to end her wait, and it was too late to change her mind.

She turned her gaze from the dusty landscape to her riding companion. The young woman sitting across from her hadn't talked much the last couple of miles, and Charlotte welcomed the change from the constant chatter that had plagued her since their introduction on the train. It had annoyed Charlotte from the moment she'd latched on with her stories and spoiled mannerisms; she doubted the girl had ever seen hard times in her life. She'd formally introduced herself many miles back as Darla Wingate, but Charlotte still hadn't shared her own name with the talkative slip of a girl whose story didn't match her appearance in the least.

Being a seamstress, Charlotte studied the rich fabric of the woman's fancy dress, the stitching like none she'd seen that were hand-sewn. How had a woman like Darla happened to become a mail-order bride? Was she in some sort of trouble, or was she simply acting like a spoiled child throwing a tantrum and running away from home? Charlotte, herself, fit the part more than this woman; a year ago, her romantic heart might have betrayed her if a man had written the sort of love-letters Darla described to her, but her heart had become too guarded since she'd been alone for so long. Charlotte envied Darla's enthusiasm in some ways. Perhaps the romance of it had drawn her in.

"Do you have family in Silver City?" Darla asked.

Family? My brother abandoned me, and both my parents are dead and buried.

Up until now, she'd carefully avoided conversation that steered toward the subject, but she couldn't continue to sidestep her answers without being rude. Despite every attempt at keeping to herself, the woman seemed determined to pull her in with her stories and her never-ending questions.

The hopeful expression lingered across Darla's dainty features as if she would wait the entire trip for Charlotte to answer. Her pa had taught her not to converse openly with strangers, but she'd learned a lot about the woman, though she hadn't yet shared even a crumb of her own story for fear she'd open a floodgate of fresh tears.

"I'm going to see my brother, Rooster," Charlotte answered, biting her bottom lip.

The lopsided grin that spread across Darla's lips warned her the conversation wouldn't end there. She'd seen that look too many times. Everyone always asked about his unusual name.

TWO

Silver City, Nevada

Rooster Figg slammed his fist down on Beau Dalton's desk. "I won't be cheated another day by you," he said through gritted teeth. "Our deal was six months at half pay in exchange for the watch and the mine, and it turned into a year. I'm leaving your employ, and I need my pa's pocket watch and that deed, now."

Beau motioned to his foreman, who un-looped the leather tie from the hammer of his gun and rested his hand on it; too often the man used his boss's power to hide behind his crimes, and if he shot Rooster, he'd take a dozen witnesses defending him when he went to the sheriff whether they saw what happened or not. The man was a fast-draw, and Rooster only carried a gun to protect himself against the occasional rattlesnake or coyote out on a cattle drive. He'd never shot a man before and he wasn't about to find out if he was capable; there was a big difference between defending against a rattlesnake and a human, and he doubted the foreman mirrored his beliefs on the issue. To shoot a rattlesnake or a human meant no difference when defending Beau Dalton; neither shot would weigh on the foreman's conscience. Rooster had learned to keep to himself, and getting away from Beau was long-overdue.

Beau smirked, resting his elbows on the blotter that spanned half the surface of the rich, mahogany desk. "Now that we have an *understanding,* I told you, saddle-tramp, that I'd mistaken the value of the land when I made the original deal with you. I'm still not convinced you've earned the full value of that mine. My men built a house out there to make improvements on the land."

"That's no house!" Rooster said, raising his voice. "We both know that's nothing more than a leaky old shack that would cost just as much to repair as it would to tear it down and rebuild."

"It's a place to hang your hat nonetheless, and you're still getting more than you earned."

"I've done the work of four men for half the wages owed one man, and I've put in more sweat and blood into this land than you have. You know just as well as I do that mine is worthless!"

It meant everything to Rooster, but he would never let on to Beau, or the price would increase. To him, it meant being able to fetch Charlotte; to Beau, it was a means of getting something for nothing.

Beau leaned back in his leather chair, his seat squeaking under his tailored suit pants. "I don't need to work this land; I own it. I have a feeling that mine means more than pure gold to you," he said, chuckling. "I think that land stands between you bringing your sister here and not. You can't have her in the bunkhouse where you're staying now, but she'd be more than welcome here in my house with me. Perhaps you'd like to stay on here and send for her after all. We could make a trade for the mine—your sister for the deed." He tipped his head back and laughed.

Rooster's pulse increased, his desire to teach Beau some respect boiled in his blood.

"I told you I'm not working another day for you," Rooster said firmly. "You and I both know I haven't drawn a bit of pay in the year that I've been here; just let me take my horse and saddle, my pa's pocket watch, and the deed you promised me, and I'll be on my way. I've paid you in full."

Beau opened the lid of a small cedar box on his desktop, pulled out a cigar and placed it in his mouth to wet the end. With a precision of patience, he picked up a small, steel cutter and pinched off the end with the round-ended scissors. Still ignoring Rooster, he rose from his chair and stepped over to the fireplace, where he drew a cedar stick from the kindling bucket and lit it with a match until it caught fire. He glanced at Rooster with a slow smile as he plucked the cigar from his lips and twirled it in the flame until it was evenly lit. He blew lightly on the embers as he rotated the cigar in his fingers until it produced a glowing ring around the tip, then he snuffed out the flaming stick and tossed it onto the coals at the bottom of the grate, leaving it smoldering there. Stuffing the cigar between his teeth, he began stoking it, blowing the smoke out the side of his lips. Once his cigar produced a level of smoke to his satisfaction, he returned to his rich, leather chair and lifted his gaze toward Rooster.

"I'm the most successful rancher in this territory, and I didn't get that way by giving away my money to drifters and saddle-tramps with no more than the shirt on their backs and a dream in their pocket of owning a piece of Nevada territory. You'll get your little cutout of land when I say you'll get it and not a moment before. I don't want it; I'm a cattleman, not a miner. I only offered that piece of rock and sand to you because I won it in a poker game myself. But you're right, it's worthless—just as worthless as you've been to me while you've been here. Worthless workers don't get good things; you'll get the old nag and that rotten saddle in the tack-room—and you can have your worthless mine, but nothing else, or you'll owe me more time!"

"That swayback horse and rotted saddle are not what you promised me for the work I did, and according to you, the mine is worthless. So, the way I see it, you got a year's worth of free work out of me."

"That's right, saddle-tramp; you *get* worthless because you *are* worthless."

He was certain Beau referred to his lack of loyalty when it came to the lack of morals he expected from his men. They pushed the letter of the law because it was expected of them and they were used to the foreman's shady orders, but Rooster had made friends with the sheriff, and he knew which side of the law he stood on. He wasn't about to change his morals or shame his ma and pa over a few silver coins jingling in his pocket at the end of the month.

He'd practically sold his soul through sweat and the strength of his back to gain the deed for the mine. He'd gladly live in the line shack out at the mine. Anything was better than being charged room and board to work for a greedy man and living in a bunkhouse with a bunch of immoral, drunkard cowpokes. He didn't know any other ranchers who charged their hands to live in the bunkhouse, but perhaps that rule had only applied to him.

"What about my pa's pocket watch?" Rooster said through gritted teeth.

He chuckled again. "I don't know why you're getting mad at me; you ought to be mad at yourself for staking it in a card game. I bet your daddy is rolling over in his grave." He pulled it from the belly drawer of his desk. "You can have this stupid pocket watch; it never worked anyway."

Rooster rose from the chair quickly, leaning over Beau's desk. "That watch worked just fine before I handed it over to you!"

The ramrod clicked back the hammer of his gun and had it trained on Rooster. He stared down the barrel of the Colt Peacemaker, deciding he'd better not challenge Beau while he was outnumbered, and slowly lowered himself back into the chair.

"Turn around, saddle-tramp," Beau grunted around the cigar clenched between his teeth. "The deed is in my safe and I don't trust you not to see the combination and rob me."

He sighed and turned his backside to Beau, but he listened intently for any sign of trouble. The man knew better than to suspect Rooster of stealing from him, but he wouldn't put it past Beau to make an accusation. As far as he reckoned, Beau had barked the order only to keep control over him just a little bit longer.

He faced the bookcases at either side of the hearth, his eyes focusing on the books that lined the shelves in Beau's den. They had a way of intimidating him with their thick spines and gold-embossed bindings, and the big words he didn't understand. He hadn't been to a formal school, and the little bit of learning his ma had tried to instill in him had gone to waste. The thick books mocked him from the shelves as though they helped their owner to gain superiority over him. He knew better; Beau was a swindler who would sooner take his own ma's money if he wanted it, but he wasn't as smart as he pretended to be.

Rooster's schooling had taken second priority even though he could read and write enough to get him by. When he was a boy, he'd been more interested in being just like his pa, and would sooner shoot tin cans and learn to rope and ride, than learning how to read and write as well as Charlotte did; now was not the time to wish he'd paid more attention to his ma's teachings. If he'd been better at reading and cyphering, Beau wouldn't have him over a barrel the way he had for the past year.

He'd needed full pay, so he could fetch Charlotte from the Barbary Coast and save her from a possible fate of having to work in a saloon just to make ends meet. Even he knew she couldn't make enough money sewing dresses for the few clients she had, and the money from the small dowry pa had insisted she keep would have only lasted her so long.

As an older brother, he'd failed her in so many ways it filled him with shame, but now was the time to put an end to that. Even if he had to make a home for the two of them from the line shack at the mine, it was better than not taking care of her at all, which is what he'd done so far. He'd been too ashamed to return her correspondence over the past year. Wouldn't she be surprised when he finally sent for her? Sure, the line shack wasn't much, but he was certain Charlotte could *lady it up* and make it feel like home.

Rooster listened and waited until after Beau slammed the heavy door to the cast-iron safe, flipped the latch and spun the dial. It made him nervous to have his back to the two men, and so he quickly turned around to face them when he was sure the man had finished.

Beau opened the flap to the deed and glanced over it for a long pause. Without looking up, he took his quill pen from the stand and dipped it in the inkwell, and then scraped a dramatic signature at the bottom of the page. He blew on the ink to dry it before closing it back over the folds. "Don't come around here asking for work when you realize what a foolish trade you've made with me; you won't be hired back," he said, sliding the deed across his desk.

"I can't afford to keep working for you!"

Beau and his foreman snickered.

Anger filled Rooster, but he knew it was better to walk away while he was still ahead. "I think I'll be happy to leave here with the same silver dollar I had in my pocket when I got here."

Rooster snatched up the deed and backed out of the room without another word; he wasn't

about to give Beau Dalton the chance to put a
bullet in his back.

THREE

Nevada Territory

Charlotte stared out the window of the stagecoach at the blurred view of the desert as they rode past, her thoughts drifting to a happier time in her life. She was eager to see her brother, but even a reunion with him wouldn't completely fill the gap in her heart.

She turned away from the passing landscape, her gaze focused on Darla, whose cheeks had become flush and her skin glistened with moisture, her breaths now shallow toils. They hadn't slept more than subtle drifting the entire trip, but her condition showed more than exhaustion.

"Are you feeling poorly, Miss Darla?" Charlotte asked, her voice raspy from the grit caking her throat.

Her head leaned to the side, resting against the back of the leather seat. "I'm fine," she said, her voice so soft Charlotte barely heard her above the rattling of the stagecoach. "I think I'd like to be quiet for a little while and just listen to you tell me a story for a change. Tell me about your brother, Rooster." She barely smiled, but her enthusiasm hadn't faltered.

Charlotte reached into her reticule for a clean handkerchief and wobbled over to the other side of the carriage, tumbling onto the seat beside Darla when the driver rounded a curve. She righted herself and then dabbed at the girl's forehead and cheeks, mopping up perspiration that had darkened her strawberry blonde hair and smudged the trail-dust coating her skin. "I think you may be a little overheated from the stifling temperature," she said. "I don't believe we're too far from the way-station; you should probably get out and stretch your legs a little once we get there."

Darla nodded slowly, as if she'd become too tired to even hold her head up any longer.

Charlotte pulled down the canteen from a hook on the wall inside the coach. The little bit of water in it had come from a pond several miles back and wasn't fit for drinking, but it would likely cool Darla's skin enough to ease her suffering in the dry heat. She uncorked the mouth of the canteen and upturned it to dampen the handkerchief, then replaced the wooden plug in the spout. Dabbing at her face with the cloth, she did her best not to alarm Darla to the possibility she may be coming down with a fever.

"Tell me about your brother," she begged, her voice becoming quiet.

Darla rested her head against Charlotte's shoulder and closed her eyes, the hopeful, half-smile still curving up her lips.

I suppose it can't hurt to share a little bit, especially if it'll make her feel better.

"When my brother was ready to be born," she began. "My ma had labored hard all night long trying to give birth to her firstborn. She'd been so weak and overtired that she couldn't keep from falling asleep in the middle of giving birth. Just before dawn, our rooster hopped onto the windowsill of the room, poked his head in and crowed. My pa said it woke my ma straight away and made my brother wail something fierce before he was fully born. For three days after his birth, he would cry every time that rooster would crow, so despite all the protesting from my ma, my pa said Rooster was the only sensible name for him—that, and he had a little tuft of reddish hair on top of his head like the rooster's comb. His whole life, he hasn't been able to sleep if there was a rooster crowing anywhere within miles of our house. I can sleep right through it, though."

She paused for a moment, relishing the memory of the story that she'd heard from her pa's lips more than once over the years. She could still hear her parents' laughter in her head. For some reason, that story became funnier every time he'd tell it, and her ma never seemed to mind that he'd embellish a little more each time; she'd go along with him, being a perfect audience, and rewarding him with a more dramatic applause than the previous telling.

A light giggle escaped Darla's lips, though her blue eyes darkened. "That's a good story."

Charlotte nodded, blinking away a tear; it was one of her fondest memories.

She touched Darla's arm lightly, noticing the silkiness of her sleeve.

"Do you sew your own dresses?" Darla asked.

The question caught Charlotte off-guard. "Yes, I do."

"I noticed you admiring my dress more than once," she said. "I'd wanted to purchase some that were a little more practical, but there wasn't time before I left San Francisco."

Charlotte was almost on the edge of her seat, waiting for her to share the reason behind her journey to be a mail-order bride. The idea was preposterous; marrying a perfect stranger was simply terrifying. Darla had been quiet for a while, but suddenly became talkative again and she didn't want to miss out on knowing her reason.

"I thought your dress looked more like it was made with one of those fancy machines with a treadle. Your dress—and the way you talk don't fit somehow. You don't look like you *need* to accept a contract with a man. I don't mean to pry, but you don't look like the kind of woman who would—I mean," Charlotte stumbled over her words.

Darla smiled. "I know what you meant, and you're right. But if I'd stayed at home, my father would have forced me to marry his business partner who's almost twice my age and I didn't love him. I'm certain my mother is making excuses for my brazen behavior to her social circles even as we speak, but I just couldn't go through with it. I had to leave."

Charlotte patted her arm. "I'm sorry; I didn't know. I don't blame you; I would have done the same thing. But aren't you taking a risk with the man on the other end of this trip? What do you know about the man you've agreed to marry?"

"Beau Dalton is a good, God-fearing man whose parents left him a working ranch outside of Silver City," she said. "His letters are filled with inspiration and kindness and he's so eager to meet me."

Anyone can be kind in a letter.

"Did you sign the marriage contract?"

Darla nodded. "I had to agree so he would send me passage. My father would never have given me that much money without needing to know why I needed it, so I had to agree to Mr. Dalton's terms. You can hardly expect a man to pay passage for a woman who might back out on their agreement once they meet."

"If the man is a deceiving scoundrel, he would certainly feel the need to have a signed contract. A man as handsome and God-fearing as your Beau Dalton claims to be wouldn't worry about you backing out once you met him!"

Darla bit her bottom lip, her eyebrows tightly knit together. "I didn't think of it that way; oh, now you have me terribly worried."

Charlotte didn't envy Darla.

"I'm afraid I acted rather hastily, but I'm afraid he isn't getting much for the bargain. I never even learned to sew," Darla said. "I can make a sampler, but I can't sew a dress like you can."

Her comment took Charlotte by surprise; she thought all women knew how to sew.

"Sewing a dress is a lot more like making a sampler than you might think, the stitching is a little different, but I suppose I could teach you."

Charlotte had no idea why she was offering such a service to the young woman. Although they would be living in the same city, she doubted they would have much to do with each other. Darla would be marrying a wealthy rancher, and Charlotte had no idea what living conditions or hardships she would be enduring with her brother, but she doubted they would mingle in the same social circles.

"I never learned how to cook, either; I have no idea how to make even the simplest of meals." Darla said quietly. "Do you know how to cook?"

Charlotte nodded. "I can teach you the basics of cooking, so you won't disappoint your new husband, but how is it that you never learned any of these things you will need to know to be a wife and have a family?"

"I'm ashamed to say that my family had a cook and a chambermaid. I would have had those things once I married Mr. Von Barron. Mother and I had our dresses specially made by a seamstress in town, and my father thought that finishing school had been more important than getting my hands dirty."

"Not even as a child, you weren't allowed to get dirty?"

Darla shook her head. "When I was young, all I wanted to do was to learn to cook; it looked like so much fun. I wanted to cook my father something special—a chocolate cake, the way Miss Betsy, our cook, always made. She had strict instructions not to allow me into the kitchen unless I was taking my afternoon meal, but I would sit there and watch her cook, and she'd allow me to take my time when I ate so I could watch her. She was a very kind woman. One afternoon, I sneaked into the kitchen and swiped a pan and some flour and sugar, and a little milk and butter because I was going to surprise my father by making him a cake just like Miss Betsy. I'd forgotten the cocoa powder, so I substituted a little bit of dirt to make it look chocolatey, thinking the sugar would make it sweet enough."

Giggles erupted from both of them.

"I did everything else the way Miss Betsy did when I watched her," Darla continued. "Then I baked it while she was busy doing the laundry in the wash-house. When my father bit into that cake I was so proud that I'd made for him, he nearly fired Miss Betsy, until I came forward and admitted I'd made it."

They both laughed.

"That sounds a little bit like my first cake; I used to love rainy days, so I could stomp in the mud."

"Didn't you suffer punishment for that?" Darla asked.

Charlotte laughed and shook her head. "I was careful not to muddy up my shoes; I used to love the feel of the mud between my toes. I always went down to the wharf afterward and washed off in the salty sea—it's the best thing for cleaning mud out of your clothes."

"I've never done that, but I've seen other kids doing it when I was younger, and I always envied their freedom to express themselves as only children can."

"I'm sorry you didn't get to experience such fun things as a child," Charlotte said. "I don't believe my pa would have been angry with me for making him a mud cake. He would have

45

laughed—and teased me about it for the rest of my life."

Darla sighed. "There had been no appreciation in my father's eyes that day, only intolerance for his only child. So, he sent me away to finishing school after the summer break. It was his way of punishing me for having a mind of my own; he said I needed *refinement*."

Charlotte smirked, but quickly covered her mouth. "I'm sorry," she said. "He used school as a punishment?"

"And a punishment it was! I learned to recite poetry, walk gracefully, and play the piano; they taught me to drink tea in the afternoon properly, and how to sit still and quietly for hours on end for no other reason than my father being present in the room."

No wonder she won't stop talking; she's got a lot of words just bursting to be spat from her mouth!

"What good is learning to have tea in the afternoon and walk and speak properly, if you

46

aren't allowed to express yourself? Those things might be important in social standing, but it's the practical things in life that add to your character. Learning to sew and to cook are both practical things that a person needs to know to survive. If I may be so bold, it sounds as if your pa wanted you to be dependent the rest of your life. What better way to please a husband than to cook him a hot meal and mend his clothes?"

"Will you really teach me those things?"

She patted Darla's arm. "I'd be happy to, but we can talk about that later. You rest until we make the stop-over, and we can talk more when you've cooled off."

Darla leaned back and closed her eyes, the sweat on her brow suggested she still suffered from the heat.

Way Station, Nevada Territory

A loud halt from the driver slowed the horses down, nearly jolting Charlotte from the carriage seat. As they pulled into the yard in front of the outpost, she took a deep breath and allowed herself to smile. It meant they could escape the confines of the Wells Fargo coach and stretch their weary muscles. They were only halfway to Virginia City, and she worried Darla may need to see a doctor. Right now, a drink of water would probably do her a lot of good, but she would keep an eye on her.

She jiggled the woman's arm just enough to wake her. "Miss Darla, we've stopped at the way-station; would you like to get out for some fresh air and some water?"

Groaning a little, her lashes fluttered. The door flung open and the stage driver held a shotgun in his right hand, the barrel pointing toward the sky and the heel of the stock resting on his hip.

"Let's go, Ladies," he said around a stick of jerky clenched between his teeth. "We're on a schedule and we need to swap out the draft horses for fresh ones; you can get something to eat inside."

She regarded his weathered face; his short beard peppered with gray and his soft eyes held a kindness about them. "Please, Sir, she could use some help getting out. She's not well; I think she's overheated from the trip."

He rested the shotgun on the ground and leaned it against the coach.

An older man approached, his scraggly, white beard stained with tobacco from the lump of chaw packed in his cheek. He spat a stream of tobacco in the dirt, squinting as he swiped his tattered hat from his wispy, white hair. He slapped the hat against his leg, a cloud of dust blowing off it in the breeze. "What've we got here?" he asked, replacing his hat.

The stage driver glanced over his shoulder. "Hey, Ole Prospector, tell your wife we're gonna need some water for this one; she ain't lookin' too spry."

The man scrambled away, his back hunched and his knees bowing out as he walked; he kicked up a cloud of dust as he shuffled toward the primitive building.

Holding his hand out, the driver assisted Charlotte down first. Then, reaching inside, he scooped Darla up in his arms, pulling her against his barrel chest and carried her inside the outpost.

Charlotte followed him, where the caretaker's wife immediately moved toward them with a pitcher of water and poured some into a glass that sat on the table in front of them. Places were already set as if they'd been expecting them, but she supposed they were always prepared because they knew the stagecoach schedule.

The stout woman helped Darla hold the cup to her lips; she winced with every swallow. After a few sips, she pushed the cup away and coughed. She rubbed her thin arms, hugging them close to her. It was a bit cooler in the tree-shaded building than it had been in the sweltering heat of the coach. Charlotte draped her shawl around the young woman's shoulders, brushing her heated skin with the back of her hand.

She glanced up at the older woman. "She's burning up with fever!"

Fear gripped her heart.

"Let's get her over to the settee so she can lie down," the caretaker's wife said, drying her hands on the apron tied at her ample waist.

They each took one of her hands and placed an arm around the middle of her back, helping her up from the chair. Darla shuffled her feet with slow, controlled steps toward the settee, her head hanging so her chin touched her chest.

After they lowered her onto the settee, the woman disappeared for a minute, reappearing with an oval, enamelware dishpan full of water, a thick piece of cheesecloth swimming in the jostling water.

She squeezed out the cloth and pressed it against Darla's cheeks and forehead, then handed it to Charlotte. "I've got to serve up some food to the menfolk; keep applyin' that cool rag to her skin and it'll help bring her fever down. I'll be back to check on her after I'm finished. What's your friend's name?"

Charlotte kept her gaze lowered. "Her name is Darla, but I suppose I hadn't really thought of her as being my friend; we only just met on the train."

The woman paused and smiled. "It seems to me if I was sick with a fever, I'd want a friend like you takin' care of me."

Charlotte grimaced as she dabbed the cool cloth on Darla's face, tears stinging her eyes, but she sniffed them back. "I only just started taking care of her the last couple of miles of the trip; she'd been so talkative that I hadn't noticed anything was wrong until she began to get a little too quiet. I'd been too wrapped up in my own worries to notice until it was too late."

"The point here is that you did notice," the woman said. "Her illness couldn't have been prevented, so, don't you go blamin' yourself; it won't do her any good if you're fallin' apart."

"Yes, Ma'am," she said. "You must think I'm awful for not thinking of her as my friend, but I'm afraid I don't really know what it means to be a friend anymore; I've kept to myself mostly for the last year or so."

It'd been so long since she'd opened up to another person, she found it difficult to do. Mrs. Billings had done everything she could to coax her out of her mourning period, but she wasn't sure if she'd ever get past losing both her parents and her brother all in the same year. Her faith finally opened her eyes to the life she was missing out on and drew her out of mourning, so she could make the long journey to be with Rooster, her only living relative.

The older woman pursed her lips, her hands resting on her hips. "We've all got our troubles, but it seems to me you know enough about friendship to give it that much thought. Tell me your name, child."

"My name is Charlotte." She chided herself for being so stingy with Darla. She could have easily told her what her name was at any time during the journey, but she hadn't been looking for friendship. She'd been too blinded by missing her brother to consider anyone's feelings but her own.

The woman smiled. "I'm Mary. You get your friend feelin' comfortable while I tend to the menfolk, and I'll bet she'll be feelin' better in no time at all."

She returned the smile, nodding obedience to the woman's request.

After Mary left the room, Darla lifted her lashes and smiled a weak smile. "I'm pleased to finally make your acquaintance, Charlotte," she said, her eyes drifting closed again.

From the other room, Mary hummed *Amazing Grace;* Charlotte joined her, remembering she'd hummed the same hymn to her ma the night she passed on to be with the Lord.

Charlotte's throat clogged with tears as she raised her eyes heavenward. *Lord, thank you for my new friend, Darla. Please make her well again.*

The aroma of fresh coffee and bacon tugged at Charlotte's heart and made her mouth water.

The bread and fruit Darla had shared with her along the trip had been an open invitation for friendship and she'd missed it. The only real thing on her mind was getting to Silver City and collecting Rooster so she could take him back home to San Francisco.

Perhaps God has a higher purpose for my journey.

FOUR

Silver City, Nevada

Rooster slid from the old mare's back and patted her neck. It had been a long trip into town since he didn't want to push the horse to her limits. If he took good care of her, she'd be worth a few more good rides before she needed to be put out to pasture. He'd left the saddle behind; there was no sense trying to cinch that heavy old broken-down saddle when it was easier on both him and the horse to ride bareback.

He grabbed the lead strap and tied it to the hitching post, and then stepped onto the boardwalk, his spurs jingling and clicking against the boards. He flipped his silver dollar between his thumb and forefinger, trying to figure out how to multiply it to cover the expense of recording the deed; not to mention, the money he would need for supplies and a pack-mule to work the mine. Then there was the money that weighed most on his mind; the money he needed for his sister.

Lord, you know my needs; please bless me with a miracle so that I can fetch Charlotte.

Distracted by his prayer, he didn't notice the drunken man stumbling out of the saloon; the plea from the preacher's wife had been what drew his attention away from his troubles.

"Let go of me," she screamed, swatting at the man with her gloved hand. Her basket of groceries fell during the struggle; apples rolled across the boardwalk and a sack of flour broke open, while half a dozen eggs cracked and spilled out.

Rooster paused, his heart racing, but he quickly stepped between the rowdy cowboy and the pale, shaky woman without another thought. He urged her to be on her way, but the man grabbed her by the arm.

"I ain't done talkin' to this pretty little filly," the man said, his breath pungent with the odor of barrel-whiskey.

"She's the preacher's wife," Rooster said, gritting his teeth. "She won't be keeping your company."

Still holding her arm, he smiled and staggered, bringing his face close to hers. "Do you think your husband can save my soul? He might need to when I'm done talking to you!" He laughed, and it only made Rooster that much more nervous. He was unarmed, and the drunken man could not be trusted not to draw on him.

How many times had his pa told him to keep his gun strapped to his waist at all times? To be ready for the unexpected. He pictured his gun tucked away in his saddlebag, slung over the horse; he would never reach it in time to defend them. He would have to use his wit and his brawn to defend.

Lord, help us both.

Rooster slapped him playfully on the shoulder. "Why don't you let me buy you a drink, *friend,"* he said, hoping to distract him. He'd only stepped foot inside the saloon once, and it wasn't for a drink, but he would spend his last silver dollar to save the preacher's wife.

The man's expression darkened; he shoved Rooster away. "Not now, I'm going to have a drink with the lady."

"I don't drink; please let me go," she cried out.

Rooster wedged himself between them again, but the man wouldn't let go of his grip on her.

"Let her go," the sheriff yelled from the end of the boardwalk.

Rooster saw the man going for his gun, so he snaked his arm around the woman's waist and kicked the drunken man away, pulling the woman down to the ground with him. Two shots were fired just as Rooster hit the boardwalk, the preacher's wife landing safely on his arm. Muffled cries filled the streets as the townsfolk gathered to witness the ruckus, but the man lay face-down in the dirt.

Rooster's gaze met with the preacher's wife's only for a moment before he helped her to her feet and then leapt across the boardwalk to get the unconscious man's gun. Sheriff Tucker was at his side within moments and bound the cowboy's wrists in irons.

The man groaned when the sheriff rolled him over. "My bullet missed him, but you knocked him out cold when you pushed him over that railing," Sheriff Tucker said. "His bullet might have hit me if you hadn't pushed him. You saved my life, Rooster."

"Mine too," the preacher's wife said from behind him. "Surely the Lord will reward you."

Sheriff Tucker chuckled. "I got a new set of dodgers when the mail came in on today's stage, and this man's face was on one of them; he's got a five-hundred-dollar bounty on his head, and you caught him, Rooster. That entitles you to the reward."

Rooster kicked at the dirt and scoffed. "All I did was push him away from the preacher's wife; I wasn't trying to catch him."

"Help me get him into the jail, and we can discuss it after we get him locked up," the sheriff said, as he glanced up at the preacher's wife. "Are you alright ma'am?"

She shooed him with her hand. "Don't you give me a second thought. You take care of your prisoner and make sure Rooster gets that reward money so he can bring his sister here; we need her for our sewing circle." With that, she stepped back onto the boardwalk and picked up her basket. The proprietor invited her back into the store to replace her ruined groceries.

Sheriff Tucker looped his arms under his prisoner's arms and hoisted him up, Rooster at his feet, and the two men carried him to the jailhouse. Once the prisoner was securely locked up, the men walked out to the office area where the sheriff grabbed two cups and filled them with coffee that warmed on the pot-belly stove in the corner. He placed one of the cups in front of Rooster and put the other on top of his filing cabinet as he rifled through the top drawer. He pulled out a handful of dodgers and tossed them onto his desk, the top poster was an exact liking of the prisoner. Sheriff Tucker lifted the outlaw's gun from his belt and set it on the desk. Inlaid with silver into the black walnut grip were the initials *FH*.

"Frank Harlow," Sheriff Tucker said, holding up his dodger. "Says he's wanted for cattle-rustling, robbery, and assault. He escaped from the territorial prison last month. The bounty is five hundred dollars, and it's all yours, my friend."

Rooster ran a hand through his thick, ruddy hair. He bit his bottom lip to control his emotions.

"Do you realize with that money I can finally send for Charlotte? I can work the mine, and fix up the line-shack, and…"

Sheriff Tucker held up a hand to calm him. "Slow down, buddy, did Dalton finally give you the deed to the mine?"

Rooster jumped up as if owning the mine was fresh news to him. "Yes!" he said with hands raised heavenward. "And I'm a free man—and a rich one! I've got to send a wire to San Francisco."

"Let's not put the cart before the horse," Sheriff Tucker warned him. "I'll have to wire the prison and have them send someone to fetch the prisoner and bring the bounty. It might be the end of the week or later before they get here. Even then, they have to properly identify him and approve the transfer."

Rooster whipped his head around. "What if it isn't him? Oh, that would be just like pulling a dream out from under me."

"It's him," the sheriff assured him. "Look at the picture on the dodger; it's him just as sure as you're Rooster Figg. The picture, and the gun with his initials; it all fits, so don't you worry. That money will be yours in just a few days."

Rooster sank into the chair with a scowl. "Did you ever want something so bad you can't hardly stand to wait for it? You know it's been like that ever since I got here. I've been waiting for the day I could send for my sister, and now it's here— except I have to wait even longer. I know I've waited over a year, but suddenly I feel like I couldn't wait even another day."

The sheriff crossed the room and replaced the rest of the *Wanted* posters into his filing cabinet. "I might be able to help you with that," he said.

Rooster crossed his arms over his chest and leaned back in the chair. "I'm listening."

"I've got enough money in the bank, so I can help you get started on that dream."

"Whoa!" Rooster said. "I pay my own way."

Sheriff Tucker slammed shut the filing cabinet. "Let go of that pride and send a wire to your sister; let her know you'll be sending a bank draft at the end of the week for her to board the train, and then you can get her a ticket she can pick up in Reno for the stagecoach. In the meantime, I'll give you enough to rent a buckboard at the livery, so you can pick up some things at the general store to spruce up the line-shack and start working the mine. I reckon that ought to keep you plenty busy until she gets here."

Rooster shook his head. "Thank you, Sheriff; that sounds all well and good, but that would probably take every last dollar you own, and I can't do that to you."

"You'll be borrowing it temporarily," the sheriff said. "I'll have that money back within a week."

"What if it takes them longer to come for the prisoner?"

The sheriff leaned back and chuckled. "Do you remember when I had that other outlaw in here until a representative from the prison came to pick him up? All the ladies from church brought me food until he was gone since I couldn't leave the prisoner alone for too long. I'm sure the preacher's wife already has the chuckwagon committee ready to take care of me this time—and you too, since you saved her life when you caught him."

Rooster laughed. "Some of those ladies are single; you should really see about courting one of 'em and getting yourself hitched."

Sheriff Tucker emptied the pot of coffee into his cup. "I'm already taken."

"By who?" Rooster asked. "Did one of those ladies manage to hog-tie you when I wasn't looking?"

Sheriff Tucker scowled at him; he knew better than to crack a joke like that. "You know I'm married to this job, but I'd consider marrying your sister—just for the sake of keeping an eye on her for you."

Rooster put his fist up to his mouth and bit down on his knuckle for a second to keep from laughing at his friend. "You know there is no one I'd rather see marry my sister, but don't you think you ought to ask *her* permission first?" he asked. "You've got *my* blessing, but she's got a mind of her own, and there ain't no changing it once it's made up."

"I've been waiting this whole year to meet her," he said. "I'd have loaned you the money a long time ago if Dalton hadn't cheated you out of everything you worked for. I know it was tough for you to leave, but working for him never did you any good."

"Isn't it against the law for him to work me for no pay?"

"Not if you agreed to his terms," the sheriff said. "A man like him can't keep inside of the law for long; sooner or later, he's bound to cross that line, and when he does, he'll be a guest in my jail."

"Good luck with that," Rooster said, dismissing him.

"Men like him always mess up, you'll see."

Rooster wished it could be that easy. If the law had been able to make the man pay him for the past year, he'd have had Charlotte here almost immediately. Truth-be-told, he was almost glad he hadn't been able to bring her here, so she wouldn't see how badly he'd failed. At least with the mine and the reward money, he had a chance to make something of himself, didn't he?

FIVE

Way Station, Nevada Territory

A loud crack of thunder brought Charlotte's drooped head upright. "Ma, where are you?" she called out into the darkness.

She shifted in the straight-backed chair, her heart racing as she grasped at her surroundings, trying to make sense of the dream.

Yes, it had only been a dream.

Trailing thunder rattled the small window in the room, and it rattled her nerves, causing her to shiver. She was so exhausted, the chair, though too uncomfortable to sleep soundly, had become just comfortable enough to cradle her weary bones long enough to doze off. She rubbed at her stiff neck, wondering what time it was. Judging by her internal clock and the number of times she'd been up with Darla; her best guess was about an hour before dawn. Whatever small fraction of time she'd slept, it had only been long enough to disorient her and make her crave more. Throughout the night, she'd consistently offered the ailing woman sips of cool water and mopped at her feverish skin. Her own skin felt flush, which worried her to her very core.

Would she ever reach Rooster in time?

Another rumble of thunder, followed by streaks of lightning that illuminated the small room, caused her to jump; it rattled her bones as if someone had walked across her grave. The little room off to the side of the gathering room of the outpost was as comfortable as any, but it wasn't home, and the loneliness deep in her gut brought to life the ghosts that had chased her on this trip.

Mary had been kind enough to offer the spare room with two narrow beds, to her and Darla, but she'd feared if she laid her head down on the soft, feather ticking mattress she wouldn't hear Darla if she should need something while she slept. It was an excuse she'd told herself to avoid the very nightmares that took control of her subconscious against her will. Thoughts of that night with her ma still caused fear to trickle down her spine. The setting was the same; all that was missing were the ones she held dear to her heart— the ones she'd never see again. Only her brother remained, but he now seemed farther away than before she'd left the Barbary Coast.

Her shoulders sagged; the trip had been longer and more unbearable than she could have imagined. Darla's illness had only prolonged her meeting with her brother, and she felt miserable for it. It was a selfish thought she'd prayed away almost every hour, along with a prayer for strength to endure what she must, and a plea for Darla's health.

How had her prayers become so misguided?

Perhaps if she felt a little more settled in her spirit things would be different in her mind now, but she'd been alone for so long, and dealing with the loss of her loved ones had taken its toll on her patience and giving heart. Selfishness and bitterness had settled in her, and no matter how much she prayed them away, she could not shake them or the sadness that went hand-in-hand with it. Mary had been right in scolding her only a few hours ago for getting her priorities in order, and now was the time to do just that.

Charlotte eased herself off the Windsor chair near the window and made her way across the cool slats of the roughly-hewn wood floor. She pulled the tattered quilt over Darla; it smelled of horses and fresh hay, but she doubted the girl minded it very much.

Her eyes popped open and it startled Charlotte.

Putting a hand to her chest, she caught her breath as if she'd run alongside a team of horses. "I'm sorry, I guess I'm a little jumpy tonight because of the storm."

"You called out for your mother—in your sleep, I'm guessing," Darla whispered.

She shrugged it off. "It was just a dream."

Darla reached for her hand. "It sounded like more than that from over here; tell me what's troubling you. I want us to be friends."

Charlotte wanted the same thing, but fears of losing her new friend held her back. "I was having a dream about my ma, that's all."

"Did you leave her back in San Francisco?"

Charlotte sighed. "In a manner of speaking, yes."

Darla stared up at her as if waiting for her to explain.

Charlotte closed her eyes, her lower lip quivering. "She's buried there."

Darla attempted to squeeze her hand. "I'm so sorry."

"Being here alone—and with the storm— well, I suppose I feel a little unsettled and anxious to see my brother."

Darla forced a half-smile. "I understand. I've been lying here with my eyes closed hoping to fool myself into thinking I was at home in my comfortable room—I always felt safe knowing my parents were just down the hall from me."

"I know what you mean."

Charlotte hadn't had that safe-feeling since her ma and pa passed away, and all the imagining she could muster wouldn't make her feel at home in this place of wilderness. She didn't know how Mary could stand it, but the woman was so old, she must have had many a hard winter to get used to it. Perhaps she would feel differently once she reunited with Rooster.

She mopped up Darla's wet hair with a clean rag, and paused, blurring her vision against the flashes of lightning streaming in through the thin curtain. "I imagine you had a grand room back home, with floral wall coverings and a large, four-poster bed with lavish quilts and weaved rugs—not the braided ones—and I bet they covered almost the entire floor. I can see you sitting in a comfortable window seat surrounded by feather pillows and cloaked in a canopy of thick draperies."

"How did you do that? Guess what my room looks like, I mean?"

Charlotte smiled. "I've been in several of the wealthy homes—to sell our wares. My ma taught me how to dip tallow candles, and we sold them to the townsfolk. It had been our contribution to the income of my family. Once I learned to sew, it helped with a regular income, but I was never commissioned to sew for the wealthy ladies because I didn't have access to a sewing machine. They wanted fancy dresses—like yours. They did like our tallow candles, so my ma and I would sell them to the people who lived in the wealthier homes in San Francisco, and I've always envied the people who lived in them."

"You shouldn't envy them; they aren't always as pleasant to live in as you would think," Darla said. "What about your father? What does he do for a living?"

Charlotte bit back tears and took a deep breath before answering. "He was a deputy for the Barbary Coast."

Darla lifted her droopy lashes. "Was?"

She lowered her head; she'd already said too much. Funny, but it was the first time she'd spoken about her parents since they'd passed, fearing she would break down uncontrollably. Darla had become her friend and she needed to talk to someone before it all burst out of her from the anger that bubbled inside her gut. She could trust Darla; after all, they were going to be living in the same town, and it would be nice to have a ready-made friend.

"My pa was a deputy for fifteen years on the Barbary Coast, and he was very close to catching the men who ran a Shanghai operation.

He got a little too close, and they beat him and shot him and left him for dead."

"I'm sorry you lost both your parents; no wonder you're so anxious to see your brother," Darla whispered.

Charlotte tucked the quilt under Darla's neck, unsure if covering her would sweat out the fever, but she couldn't let her shiver. She worried about Darla, fearing if her fever didn't break soon they might lose her. "You sleep now," she said quietly.

Her ma had burned with the same fever-soaked skin that night; she hadn't made it through to see the sun rise. She hadn't been able to save her ma that night, but she would do everything she could to ensure Darla didn't suffer the same fate. Her pa hadn't been able to live without her ma, and his death proved it. The doctor suggested her pa had suffered from exhaustion during the weeks that followed her ma's funeral, and that it had caused him to become careless at his job. If he'd truly known her pa, he might have diagnosed his death from a broken heart. He wouldn't have taken the chance he did that night if her ma had still been alive—the chance that ended his life. She'd seen the same sadness in her brother's eyes the day they buried their ma, and again at their pa's burial. Was it possible his lack of correspondence had been due to illness or something *worse?*

Lord, please quiet my anxious heart until I meet up with Rooster in Silver City, and bless Darla to make a full recovery. Strengthen her so we can get her to the doctor in Virginia City in the morning.

Charlotte grabbed a galvanized pan from the corner of the room when the heavy rain began to leak through the wood-shingled roof. A chill in the air made her shiver, her aching muscles making her groan as she bent to put the pan on the floor to catch the drips. Crossing the room, she tucked the back of her hand in Darla's neck trying to judge her temperature without a doctor to measure it with a medical instrument. The first and only time she'd seen such an instrument was the night they'd lost her ma. Despite the special medical supplies and medicines the doctor had carried in his black bag, he had been helpless to postpone her meeting with the Lord.

Perhaps it would be better if she didn't know the truth of Darla's condition or it would cause her to worry more than she already had.

She dipped her hand into the oval basin on the bedside table, retrieving the wet cheesecloth and squeezed away most of the cool water. Unwinding the thin mesh, she dabbed at Darla's skin while she slept peacefully.

Her meeting with Rooster would have to wait another day. He'd let more than a year slip by without sending for her, but her conscience would not allow her to leave Darla's side for her own selfish wants.

Uncomfortable did not properly describe what went through Charlotte's mind as she wedged herself in the bed of the buckboard next to Darla. She'd chosen her hat with the widest brim, and propped a parasol over the girl's face to protect them from the early morning sun that burned through her dress. Mary's husband, the *prospector,* had loaded Darla into the wagon after Mary had lined it with old quilts and a layer of horse blankets to ensure she would be comfortable for the trip to Virginia City to visit the doctor.

Cramped between their trunks and her outstretched friend, Charlotte drew her knees to her chest and draped her long skirt over her legs. She would relax once the doctor took over Darla's care and not a moment beforehand.

The ride to Virginia City stretched on for miles of dusty trail, and Charlotte feared the blazing hot sun would only make Darla overheat again. They'd filled canteens before leaving the outpost and Mary had packed some food for the stopover at the halfway point.

Darla reached for her hand.

"Do you need a drink?" Charlotte asked.

"Yes," she said barely above the rattling of the buckboard. "I'm sorry to be such a burden."

Charlotte swallowed a lump in her throat. "You're not a burden. I stayed behind willingly to help you; I could have just as easily taken the stagecoach, but it was more important that I stay with you."

"Thank you."

Charlotte uncorked the canteen and placed a hand under Darla's head to help her drink from it. A bump in the trail caused her to spill some down the girl's neck.

"I'm so sorry," she squealed, trying to mop it up.

Darla smiled. "It's nice and cool; I liked it."

"I should be more careful or there won't be enough to last the trip."

Mary turned around. "You two ladies alright back there," she hollered over the jostling harnesses and the pounding of the horses' hooves in the dirt trail.

Charlotte smiled and nodded.

Her head ached, but she would draw on the strength of the Lord to get her through.

SIX

Silver City, Nevada

Rooster stepped up to the telegraph window just as the operator opened for business. The street already bustled with townsfolk conducting their business, but for Rooster, today was a special day—the day he could proudly send for his sister.

"I'd like to send a telegram to the Barbary Coast," he said.

The older man raised an eyebrow from over the top of his wire-rimmed spectacles. "Are you finally sending for your sister now that you've got that reward money?"

Rooster smirked. "News travels fast in this town."

"I ran into the preacher and his wife in the dining room at the hotel last night; she's telling everyone what a hero you are and how you should be the new deputy. Ever since Buck ran off and got hitched, this town's been without a deputy, and we need that for our peace of mind. This town needs you."

Rooster waved his hands furiously. "No, Sir, I want nothing to do with being a deputy."

The only reason he'd been able to help the sheriff was because his pa had always taught him and Charlotte to be on their guard; maybe if his pa had taken his own advice, he'd still be alive.

The man clicked his tongue as he wagged his head back and forth. "Folks around here are saying you're a hero for saving the sheriff and the preacher's wife. It'd be a big disappointment if you turned your back on what seems to be a natural ability for you."

"I'm no hero," Rooster said. "I saw that the outlaw had the drop on the sheriff and I had his back—that's all there was to it. I did what any man would do for a friend."

The old man cinched up his mouth and furrowed his brow as he slid a sheet of paper and a pencil across to Rooster. "Seems to me that a man ought to follow his natural calling. This town has been minus a deputy for too long, and it's getting so the folks of this town don't feel safe walking down the street no more."

Rooster tried to pen his message on the paper the best he could since his writing skills were lacking, but the man's chatter disturbed his train of thought. "I have no *calling* to be a lawman. Sheriff Tucker has several men who applied as deputy; it's only a matter of time before he chooses one, and it won't be me."

He finished his message and flipped a silver dollar onto the top of the page and walked away, a sudden heaviness clouding up his sunny day.

Rooster clicked his spurs along the boardwalk as he made his way to the General Store. The open door invited him to walk in out of the hot morning sun, the scent of spices and candles bringing thoughts of Charlotte to his mind.

"Well, if it ain't our town hero in the flesh!" the store owner said.

Rooster groaned inwardly.

The older gentleman stood behind the counter lined with tall glass jars filled with different colored candy sticks and other confections, "I heard you were gonna be our new deputy," the man continued, straightening the jars.

"You heard wrong. I happened to be in the right place at the right time, but let me put your mind at ease right now; I ain't taking Buck's place as the new deputy."

He stopped fussing with the jars, his jaw momentarily slack. "But this town really needs someone like you to help the sheriff; it's gotten so bad that folks in this town are afraid to go out during broad daylight for fear of getting shot down in the street."

Did everyone in town have a meeting last night and decide how they were going to talk me into taking the deputy position?

"I think everyone can feel just as safe as they ever did roaming the streets," Rooster commented. "Nothing's changed. In fact, it's safer now that the last of the Harlow gang is headed back to the territorial prison at the end of the week."

The proprietor swished a feather-duster frantically along the shelf behind him, all the while keeping an eye on the door. "He's already escaped once. What's to stop him from escaping again and coming back for revenge? I reckon you'll be the first one he'll come looking for."

Rooster hadn't thought about that. He shifted from one foot to the other and raked his fingers through his thick hair. He could feel his heart pounding against his ribcage as if it was trying to escape. Would he be gunned down the same way his pa had? Maybe it would be better if he left town for a while—at least until the guards came to pick up the outlaw. If he was lucky, the man had been too liquored-up to remember him if he saw him again, but Rooster wasn't willing to take that chance.

The proprietor stopped dusting his shelves and paused to look at Rooster. "What can I get for you, today?"

He stood there for a moment trying to decide what he needed to do, forgetting all about the mine; it was the last thing on his mind at the moment. "I changed my mind. I think I need to ride into Virginia City for some things."

The store owner frowned. "It'll cost you twice as much than it will in my store."

Rooster nodded. "Maybe so, but I think I need to go anyway."

The man shrugged and went back to work on the shelves. "It's your nickel," he said over his shoulder.

Rooster stepped back onto the boardwalk, the sun blinding him temporarily. Beau's foreman and five of the hands dismounted and blocked his path. He wasn't in the mood for a fight, but he half-expected it now that he was no longer in Beau's employ.

"Well if it ain't the new town hero!" the foreman said. "You ran off yesterday with your tail between your legs, and then come into town and take down an outlaw? I think you've been holding out on us for the past year. I might be able to get Beau to hire you back."

"Get out of my way, ramrod," Rooster said. "I wouldn't work for Beau again even if he paid me!"

The foreman stood his ground, and the others closed the space between them.

"There's no need to be hostile," the foreman said. "We could use a man who can hold his own—in times of *trouble.*"

"I don't care for that kind of trouble," Rooster answered, inching his way to the side.

"Where are you runnin' off to? We heard about your good fortune," one of them said. "Why don't you buy us a drink, *friend.*"

"He don't go in the saloon," another one said. "He thinks he's better than we are!"

He crowed at Rooster. They'd done it for the past year as a means to tease and intimidate him. "You better pray the rest of that Harlow gang don't come lookin' for you!"

"You ain't a hero," another one said. "You're a chicken—your pa should have named you *Chicken!*"

Rooster side-stepped to get out of their way; he wasn't going to let them intimidate him today. He had only one thing on his mind. To get out of town. He wasn't going to let these men stop him. He reached for the braided lanyard and led his mare toward the livery, Beau's men cackling and crowing to get a rise out of him that he refused to give in to.

SEVEN

Virginia City, Nevada

Charlotte packed the few things she'd removed from one of her trunks, which were out in the hall waiting for the Widow Colton's grandson to bring them downstairs for her. She would have to return for them once she rented a carriage at the livery.

Back in the quaint little room she'd shared with Darla, she crossed to the window and peered out into the street, wondering how Silver City would compare to this busy place. Even though she'd been there less than a day, she was sad to leave. She'd become attached to Darla; it was almost like having a sister. At least she supposed. Rooster was independent; they'd grown apart, and things hadn't been the same since they were children. But it would be different with Darla there; they would be living in the same town, and she wouldn't feel so alone—despite her brother's free spirit.

"You're going to wear out that window pane," Darla said from across the room.

Charlotte turned around and looked at her friend; she was snuggled up in the softest quilts the Widow Colton could find. "What do you mean?"

"You've spent most of your time here staring out at the town," she said. "I'd be willing to bet you didn't sleep a wink last night."

"I suppose a part of me doesn't want to leave here," she said. "This place is the closest I've felt to home since we started this trip. It's not near as loud and rowdy as the Barbary Coast, but it's *homey*."

Darla shifted the feather pillow under her head. "You're going to be too tired to hold your head up when you finally get to see your brother after all this time."

"I was too excited to sleep—and a little nervous; part of me fears he won't be there—that I'll find another grave to visit and the trip will be for nothing. Surely, I would have *felt* it if something was wrong with him—wouldn't I? I wouldn't be so anxious if I'd heard any word from him in the past year other than the first letter telling me he'd settled in Silver City. It's the last stop for me; if he's not there, I don't know what I'll do. There isn't anything in San Francisco to go back to."

Darla sat up in the bed. "You'll stay with me and Beau until you get on your feet, that's what you'll do!"

Charlotte crossed the room and sat on the edge of the bed. "I can't stay with you; you're going to be a newlywed, and you'll be starting a family, and I'll only get underfoot."

"If nothing else, you can come back here and stay; the Widow Colton would be happy to have you."

Charlotte nodded. "It's at least a backup plan. She told me she has a married son—her grandson's parents, and they live half way between here and Silver City. They come here to church every Sunday, so I'd have a chance to meet them. They seem like such nice folks from what she described, I suppose I could be happy here if I had to be. In a town like this, I could easily get work as a seamstress."

"Yes, and I'm sure the Widow Colton would be more than happy to help you until you got on your feet."

Charlotte sighed. "Oh, here I am making plans as if I'm never going to see Rooster again."

Darla smiled. "He'll be there; he has to be, so you and I can continue to be friends."

Charlotte returned the smile. "I'm sure we'll always be friends—no matter where we are."

She hugged Darla, tears stinging her eyes. "I'm so glad your fever broke last night, but I'm not happy you have to stay in bed for a few days. I don't want to go to Silver City without you."

Darla forced a smile as she wiped away her own tears. "It's going to be a long few days here without you, but I'll be there as soon as I feel strong enough. Don't forget to look up Mr. Dalton for me and tell him I've been delayed, but please don't tell him I've fallen ill; I wouldn't want him thinking I'm not strong enough to marry. I've come all this way, and couldn't possibly go back home."

She squeezed Darla's hand. "I'll be careful what I say, but what should I tell him if he asks why you stayed behind."

Darla winced. "I'm not sure. I suppose you could tell him I wanted to rest from the trip— which isn't a lie, and that I wanted to do some shopping for a new dress before I meet him—

which is also not a lie, because I plan to do just that as soon as the doctor will let me up out of this bed."

They giggled.

"I'll tell him, but don't push yourself to come before you're ready; listen to the doctor and make sure you're completely well before you make that trip. I know it isn't far compared to how far we've already traveled, but you want to be fresh for your Beau Dalton on your wedding day."

She nodded. "I'll see you soon. You have a safe trip to Silver City," she said, her voice a little weak. "The doctor is going to take good care of me, and I'll be there before you know it. I can't wait to meet your brother."

She tucked the quilt in around Darla's neck, happy that she no longer burned up with fever. "I'm going to tell him all about you when I get there so he'll be just as eager to meet you, too."

She smiled once more and then picked up her valise that sat next to Darla's at the end of the bed and left the room quietly.

Outside, the music of birds chirping their happy songs and the townspeople bustling about their business filled the morning air. The livery stood at the end of the boardwalk where the Widow Colton told her she could rent a carriage. She walked slowly, stopping to peek into the window of the General Store. In the window display, she admired an elegant pink dress, making a mental note of the style. She could make a dress similar once she was settled, but she wondered if she would have anywhere to show off such a fancy dress in a mining town. She had no idea what Silver City would be like, but she hoped it would be similar to Virginia City. This western town was certainly quieter than the Barbary Coast, but it was still a little bit rowdier than she would have liked. Thankfully, she had not had to stay alone in the busy city last night and would have her brother near once she made it to Silver City.

Lord, please let Rooster have a place for me when I show up, and please don't let him be angry with me for traveling all this way without his permission.

Like it or not, he was her authority with their parents gone; not that she was a child, by any means, but she had no one else to care for her. So why did she still feel so alone?

Take away my fears, Lord, and change my attitude so that when I see my brother I won't be tempted to share my disappointment with him. Help me to forgive him for neglecting me this past year.

The livery owner hitched up a large black horse to a black carriage; it made her a little nervous, as if she was attending a funeral. "Now you watch his temperament, Miss. If he tries to give you any trouble you holler the word *sugar* at him, and he'll slow right down. I give him a little bit of sugar when he behaves, but he likes to run, this one does. Only problem is, I don't have another horse here that's broke to wear a harness." He patted the horse's neck and ran his hand through his mane. "You be good for this little lady and I'll give you some sugar when they return you from the other side." He spoke kindly to the animal as if he understood him, and Charlotte hoped he could.

He assisted Charlotte onto the seat and handed her the reins. "He understands *whoa,* but don't pull on the bridle because it'll make him bite down on the bit, and he'll only run faster to make you stop."

She took the reins, but couldn't help feeling a little intimidated by the large gelding, who stamped his hoof in the dirt like he was impatient to run.

"Are you sure you wouldn't rather give me a smaller horse?" she asked.

"He's all I've got unless you want to wait a day or two and see if I get another one back in."

The last thing she wanted to do was wait another minute to be on her way to reunite with her brother.

"No, thank you," she said. "I suppose he'll have to do. Can you tell me how to get to Silver City?"

He pointed toward the far end of town.

"Follow that road all the way till it turns into a city. If you stay on the trail, Abacus knows the way; just let him lead."

"Why do you call him *Abacus?*"

The old man chuckled. "Because he's a horse you can count on. Do you get it?"

She laughed nervously. She got it, but just what it was she could count on the horse to do, she wasn't sure, so she prayed it he would get her there quickly but safely.

She tapped the reins lightly on his back to get him moving at a slow pace toward the boarding house to retrieve her trunks, and she could live with that. Yes, it meant it might be sundown before she made it to Silver City, but at least she wouldn't have to threaten the poor animal with missing out on his treat if he should misbehave and exercise his own mind on this trip. She turned around and waved to the livery owner. "Thank you."

He nodded once. "Let him lead," he reminded her. "He knows the way."

She faced forward in the seat and kept a loose grip on the reins, remembering what he'd said about not forcing him to bite down on the bit.

Lord, I thank you in advance for my safety on this trip, and I thank you for guiding this beast to get me there.

Rooster had traveled half way to Virginia City before he veered off the trail toward the Colton farm, where he intended to leave his sway-backed mare. They would give her plenty of room to roam, and she'd be able to live out the rest of her life grazing instead of being worked to death. They were kind folks—farmers, who were members of the church. Mrs. Colton would be very happy to learn that Charlotte would be arriving soon; she'd asked about her every Sunday.

The corners of his mouth curled up as he thought of his reunion with his sister, but he found himself scowling just as quickly. She was all the family he had now, and if it weren't for the sheriff reminding him Charlotte was of marrying age, he'd probably be a little more excited. He wasn't eager to bring her to the city, so she could marry up with some rowdy cowpoke. Perhaps he would have to start searching for a husband for her. Sheriff Riley Tucker was at the top of his list, and only because they were friends, but he worried about his sister spending lonely nights while he was working just like their ma had every time his pa took his post. He didn't relish the idea of his sister lying awake at night worrying if her husband would be shot down on his job.

He sighed. *Lord, why didn't you give me a brother?*

Abacus squealed and reared his front legs, snorting at the rattle snake on the side of the trail. The carriage bucked and nearly threw Charlotte from the seat. She screamed, but the animal squealed and reared again, nearly tipping the carriage over.

"No, boy, no—stop!"

She tried to steady the reins without pulling too hard, but the animal had been spooked, and it was too late to calm him. She slapped the reins prompting him to move away from the snake, and move he did. The carriage teetered and swerved as the horse set off at a gallop from start.

"Stop—bad horse—whoa," she cried out.

Terror claimed her; she could hardly breathe as she braced her foot and leaned back on the reins, hoping it would stop the horse. He only went faster. Landscape flew by, dust clouding her vision, tears streaming down her face as she bellowed another plea for the horse to stop.

"Whoa, horse, stop—please stop!" she cried.

Charlotte's seat slid from side to side, and her arms felt as if they would give out from trying to control Abacus. She felt every bump in the trail, her seat rising so often she was nearly thrown.

"SUGAR!" she finally screamed.

Abacus locked his front legs, his back legs sliding in the dirt. The carriage teetered and lurched forward, catching air under the rear wheels. Charlotte screamed and tried to brace herself inside the small coupe of the carriage, but the horse's sudden halt tossed her out onto the trail. She rolled into the scrub, toppling head over heels down the embankment, dizzying her as her vision met with the sky, then the brush, and back to the sky overhead several times until she finally stopped rolling. She tried to sit up, but couldn't; her head ached, and dizziness overwhelmed her. The sun burned her skin, but she could not move.

Back up on the road, she could hear the horse leaving her at a slow canter. "Abacus," she cried. "Stop, please stop—sugar."

It was no use; the horse was leaving, and she was too dizzy and sore to move fast enough to make her way back to the trail and stop him.

"Help!" she cried. "Lord, send me help!"

EIGHT

Silver City, Nevada

Sheriff Tucker noticed the empty carriage right away when the horse trotted in on the main street at the far edge of town. If he wasn't mistaken, that was a carriage from the Virginia City livery. He ran down into the street to catch the wayward horse before he ran over someone.

"Whoa, boy," he said as he grabbed for the lead straps. He patted the horse's lathered side; he breathed hard and snorted several times, shaking his head from side to side.

He'd been run hard and was lathered up. Sheriff Tucker walked him down to the livery so he could be taken care of properly. He needed a good rub-down and some water once he cooled down.

"Steady, boy," the sheriff said as he called out for the livery owner.

The stable boy, the proprietor's young charge, came running out of the barn. "What can I do for you, Sheriff?" he asked, before he noticed the lathered horse.

He didn't wait for an explanation, but went to the horse and wiped at his neck, talking in a soothing tone to the animal before moving to unhitch him from the carriage. He looked up at the sheriff. "What happened?"

He peered into the carriage. "I don't know, but I aim to find out; the passenger might have been thrown; I better ride on down the trail to look for him—*her!*" he said, after he noticed the reticule on the floor of the carriage.

He reached inside the carriage and plucked it from the floor; he held it up to his nose, breathing in the flowery scent for a moment as if he had a connection to it. He shook away the thought. "Can I get another horse to hitch to this carriage? I better look for her; she could be hurt and alone."

The boy nodded. "Take Ginger out of the corral in back; I just put her out so she's fresh."

The sheriff ran through the barn and out to the corral; he patted the horse and then guided her out to the waiting carriage.

"Let's go, girl, I think we've got a lady-in-distress to hunt down." He worked quickly to hitch the horse, and then hopped in and turned the carriage around, heading it in the direction it had come from. He kept Ginger at a slow trot, scanning the trail, frustrated at not finding anything.

Ginger snorted, slowing her pace; she nickered and slowed even more. "What is it, girl?" the sheriff asked, as he scanned the trail in front of him, noticing buzzards circling up ahead.

He let Ginger lead him a little further down the trail where he happened upon a woman staggering amongst the scrub along the side of the trail. Her hat had tipped to the side of her head, the feather plumes broken in half and flopping with every step she took; her dress dirty and torn at the hem and shoulder.

He halted the horse and set the brake before hopping down onto the road. Closing the space between him and the woman, he called out to her before approaching, trying not to spook her.

"Miss, do you need help?" he asked.

Charlotte jumped when he spoke, gasped, and put a hand to her chest until her eyes focused on the badge pinned to his vest.

She reached out her arms toward him awkwardly—almost as if she hadn't seen him, though he knew she had. He couldn't help but notice that even under all the dirt and scrapes how naturally beautiful she was.

"Do you know where you are, Miss?"

She shook her head, her eyes filling with tears.

"I'm lost!" she said, her voice scratchy.

"Can you tell me your name?" he asked.

She looked at him blankly and coughed.

She needed a drink of water to wash down the dirt, and in his haste, he hadn't thought to bring a canteen. If he could coax her into the carriage without spooking her, he could take her a little further down the trail to where a narrow creek crossed the path.

"Miss, I'm the sheriff of Silver City, and I'd like to help you," he said as gently as he could. He wanted to hold her up because her legs wobbled, and her head was bleeding, but he didn't want to upset her and make her think he was making improper advances. "There's a creek up ahead where we could get a drink of water; we could walk there if you think you're up to it—or we can take the carriage. Is that the carriage you rented in Virginia City?"

He worried that if the heat didn't get her, the spot on her head that was bleeding might, but he didn't want to alarm her and throw her into worse shock than she already suffered.

She looked at the carriage and shook her head. "That's not the horse; he was black and…"

Her voice trailed off and she walked a few feet beside him without speaking, until she began to collapse. He reached out and caught her before she fell, scooping up her tiny frame into his arms. He tucked her close to his chest; underneath all the dirt, she smelled just as heavenly as the reticule she'd dropped onto the floor of the carriage.

She lifted her head from his shoulder, her lashes fluttering, her eyes glassed over.

"Rooster," she whispered. Her eyes fluttered closed and she collapsed against his shoulder.

NINE

Silver City, Nevada

Sheriff Tucker slapped the reins against Ginger's flank. "Can't you go any faster?" he hollered over the clip-clop of her hooves on the hard-packed dirt on the trail.

The horse snorted and whinnied.

He blew out a discouraging breath as he looked down at the young woman leaning against his shoulder. She needed a doctor, and she especially needed to get out of this heat. He steered the horse off the road just before the covered bridge and parked the carriage in the grass in front of the creek. He carefully slid out from under her head and leaned her against the side of the carriage. Then he jumped down and pulled his bandanna from around his neck and knelt at the creek bed, dipping it in the water. He rung it out only slightly and brought it over to the carriage; he pressed it to the young woman's face and neck, but she didn't even stir. He ran back to the creek and soaked his bandanna one more time, and when he returned to the carriage he repeated the process, hoping it would cool her skin.

He gazed upon her milky skin, her cheeks pink from the heat. She certainly was angelic, but he sensed something familiar about her. She almost looked like Rooster—but only—*pretty!*

"Are you Charlotte?" he whispered to her.

She didn't answer.

"Whoever you are, I'm going to protect you."

He wished he had something to carry water in, so we could offer her a drink, but he didn't, so all he could do was get her back to town as quickly as possible. He climbed back up in the carriage next to her and tucked his arm around her to hold her up. Then he slapped the reins to turn Ginger around, so they could go over the bridge and into town.

If his suspicions were correct, the young woman sitting beside him could be none other than Charlotte Figg, and that would make her Rooster's sister. As far as he was concerned, that put him in charge of keeping her safe, not just because he was the sheriff, but because she might be the sister of his best friend.

She shifted in her seat a little after they hit a rut in the road. She let out a little gasp and tucked her arm across his chest. His cheeks heated, and he was glad she couldn't see him blushing like a school boy. He was certain that if she was awake, she would never cuddle with him, especially not in public.

He took hold of her hand and moved her arm back down to her side, the warmth of it making his skin prickle all the way up to his elbow. It put a smile on his face when she moved her arm back where she had it. Three more times he moved her arm down to her side, but she returned it across his chest. Was she awake and playing a game with him? He was only trying to keep the appearance of propriety for her sake, but she was determined to cuddle with him and he couldn't deny that he enjoyed it. He'd never taken a carriage ride with a beautiful woman or had the good fortune of having his arm around her, much less, to have her cuddle him back. Admittedly, he could get used to this feeling, but if Rooster saw him now, he'd likely frown over such bold actions—even if it wasn't intentional.

He drove the carriage into the center of town, and all eyes of the townsfolk were suddenly on him. He was certain they were curious as to why he had such a handsome woman draped over him, but more than that, he was certain they were chomping at the bit to know who she was—probably more-so than he was.

"Hey, Sheriff," the blacksmith called out to him. "I see you finally got yourself a fine-lookin' woman there; did she pass out from your boring company?"

He threw his head back and laughed, but the sheriff flashed him a disapproving look.

They'd been friends for a lot of years, so he would let the comment go for now; his only concern was getting *Charlotte* to see Doctor Goodwin.

He pulled the buggy up in front of the doc's office and before he could lift the young woman from the carriage, it seemed like half the businessmen on the street had come over to see what he was doing.

He cradled the woman in his arms. "Step aside so I can get her to the doc," he said impatiently.

"Who is she?" Willy, from the General Store, asked.

"I don't know," the sheriff answered. "But I'll let you know just as soon as I know anything. I found her down the road between here and Virginia City and she was thrown from her carriage."

"I'll ask around and see if anyone was expecting someone to visit," Willy said. "Maybe someone here knows her and can tell you who she is."

"That's a good idea," the sheriff said as he pushed through the crowd to get into the doctor's office.

Doctor Goodwin met him at the door.

He followed the doc into his office and to the back where he could treat her wounds. As he set her down on the exam table, he pulled his arms out from under her wisp of a figure and paused. He had no idea why, other than the fact he suspected she was Charlotte, but he desired to place a gentle kiss on her warm, pink cheek. He knew better of it, so he cleared his throat and stepped back so the doctor could begin his assessment. He had no idea where the urge to kiss her had come from; it had snuck up on him. He'd never felt such an unusual urge, but he had to admit, it was an exhilarating feeling. Probably wouldn't be after he felt the sting from the lady's slap across his face for being so forward. Best to put it out of his mind and leave her with the doc.

The sheriff watched through the crack in the door while Doc Goodwin and his nurse cleaned and dressed the woman's scrapes, but when Doc asked his nurse to remove the girl's dress and corset, so he could examine her ribs, that's when he decided it was best he waited outside with the rest of the crowd that had gathered outside the office.

"Can you tell us anything about her?" The hotel manager asked.

Sheriff Tucker shook his head; he wasn't about to let on to any of them his suspicion that she was Charlotte for two reasons. First one being that Rooster was out of town, and the second reason, he didn't want to put hope in any of the townspeople who'd been rooting for her arrival.

Unless she woke up and told him who she was, as soon as Rooster returned from the Colton farm tomorrow, the question of her identity would be cleared up one way or the other.

While he waited for the doc to finish, he hopped up in the carriage, so he could return it to the livery. He picked up the reins and that's when he noticed her reticule on the floor. He reached for it remembering how its heavenly feminine scent matched the young woman's. Though he was tempted to bury his face in it, he set it down beside him on the seat of the carriage and pulled away from the front of the doctor's office, turning the carriage around in the street and heading back toward the livery.

After he pulled up to the building, the stable boy came rushing out to help him.

"I heard you found the lady," he said.

Sheriff Tucker shook his head and chuckled. "News sure travels fast in this town."

"I only know because Willy is going around and asking everyone if we were expecting anyone in town. As far as I know, no one knows who she is and no one's expecting her. You might try the saloon; she might've been on her way there to get a job."

The sheriff furled his brow and sighed heavily. "I'll have you know, she isn't that kind of woman."

The young boy chuckled. "How do you know this if you don't even know her name?"

Sheriff Tucker pursed his lips and frowned.

"I just know, that's all. Besides, she wasn't dressed the part."

The boy smiled. "So, she's a refined lady, is she?"

The sheriff picked up her reticule from the seat and turned it toward his nose, his back to the young boy. "I'd have to say she is definitely a lady, and one of the finest there is."

The young boy chuckled again. "Sheriff, you weren't gone long enough to fall in love with that lady, but the way you're talking, it sure sounds like you're swooning over her."

Sheriff Tucker whipped his head around and glared at the boy. "That's none of your business, I'd appreciate you keeping your comments to yourself."

The boy hid his smile as he went around to the rear of the carriage. "There's a couple of trunks and a carpet bag back here; do you suppose they belong to your lady?"

"She's not *my* lady," the sheriff snapped without meaning to.

The boy laughed at him as he showed him the trunks. "You keep telling yourself that."

He looked at her things, and thought how lucky he'd be to have such an angelic creature love him.

"I'm going to take her things down to the doctor's office where I imagine she'll be staying until she's well enough to be moved. I'll bring the carriage right back."

When he returned to the office, the crowd was still there; he was certain by the looks on their faces they wondered what he was up to, but he wasn't in the mood to be questioned. He was the sheriff, after all, and he could do whatever he wanted—within reason.

"I hadn't realized she had luggage," he said, as he went around the back of the carriage and began to unload her trunks.

"Maybe she has something in her luggage that could identify her," Willy said.

He looked at the General Store keeper. "I'm guessing no one in town was expecting anyone who fits her description."

"None so far," Willy said. "But I put the word out, so it won't take long for it to reach everyone."

The sheriff knew how true that was, and that wasn't always a bad thing. "I'll look in her things if she isn't able to tell us who she is when she wakes up—and if no one comes to claim her."

He hoped no one would come to claim her—unless it was a family member.

He placed the carpet bag on top of the smaller trunk and went toward the door of the doc's office, and then turned around. "Can someone please take that carriage back to the livery? I've got to get in there to see if she's awake, so I can make sure there was no foul play in what happened to her out on the trail—she could have been bushwhacked."

Willy looked at him funny. "They didn't take her things!"

"She could have been carrying money! Just take the carriage back—please!"

"I'm going," Willy said, waving a hand at him.

Inside the office, away from the heat of the street, he set her things down. Doctor Goodwin came from the exam room, the expression on his face worrying the sheriff.

"What is it, Doc?" he asked.

She's in and out of consciousness, but I haven't been able to get anything out of her," Doc said. "I'm afraid she doesn't know who she is."

"I can send a telegram to the livery in Virginia City and see if they can tell me what name she gave when she rented the carriage."

"Good thinking," Doc said.

"When will I be able to talk to her?" the sheriff asked.

"She's resting now, but she should be able to talk in a few hours. I'm sure you're just as eager to get to the bottom of this as she is," the doc said. "She seemed quite disturbed that she couldn't remember her name or what happened to her on the trail. She seems traumatized."

The blood drained from the sheriff's face.

"She wasn't—um—um."

"Compromised?" Doc finished the sentence for him. "No evidence of that. Her clothing was perfectly intact."

He let out a breath with a whoosh. "What was she thinking going out alone on that trail? She could have been killed!"

"Just don't tell her that when she wakes up." Doc warned him. "I don't want my patient anymore stressed than she already is. Maybe she'll remember everything when she wakes up and this mystery will all be solved. She's suffered a concussion, though, so it could be days or weeks before she fully recovers."

The door to the doctor's office burst open and in walked Beau Dalton, his foreman and another hand with him. "Where is she?" he asked.

"Where is who?" the sheriff asked.

"The young woman you brought here."

"What do you want with her?" Sheriff Tucker asked.

"I'm here to claim her," Beau said. "She's Darla Wingate, my mail order bride!"

TEN

Virginia City, Nevada

Rooster walked into the entrance to the boarding house to see the Widow Colton. He'd spent the night at the Colton farm in the barn—trying to waste time or buy himself some time—he wasn't sure which, just as long as he stayed away until the prisoner was safely back at the territorial prison.

She greeted him with a smile. "Mr. Fick," the widow said.

It's Figg, he thought to himself. She'd called him *Fick* ever since she'd met him, and he'd tried to correct her at first, but her hearing was so bad, he didn't have the heart to continue to correct her. He'd never once offered his first name to her, thinking it wouldn't be any easier for her.

"What brings you into the city? It's not Sunday already, is it?"

"No ma'am," he said. "I came to make a delivery from your son; I stayed over in their barn last night and swapped horses with them. He gave me a good deal if I promised to make this delivery to you, so here I am."

She rubbed her hands together and smiled eagerly peering out the door around him. "What did you bring me?"

"I've got a couple dozen eggs, a couple of roasting hens, some freshly churned butter, a three gallon can of milk, and a basket full of fresh vegetables from your daughter-in-law's garden."

The Widow Colton's eyes brightened like those of a little child's when offered a stick of candy. It did Rooster's heart a good turn to help the widow in any way he could. The Colton family had been very good to him since he'd been in Nevada and his visit with Henry Colton had given him a good idea. Knowing that his friend's mother was getting on in years, he intended to offer Charlotte as a helper at the boarding house. Not only would Charlotte need the job, but he'd been selfish thinking that she would be happy with him out at the line shack.

"I'm so glad you brought me all these things," she said. "And they arrived just in time; I have a guest staying here. A young lady from San Francisco; she arrived yesterday with another young lady, but she left for Silver City this morning. Now I can't recall either of their names, because you know my memory just isn't what it used to be, but I think the two of you would have a lot to talk about. Didn't you tell me you were from San Francisco?"

Rooster chuckled. "You are close; I actually came from the Barbary Coast, but they are both in the same place. Let me get the things unloaded for you and then I'll be on my way. I could use a bath and shave and I'd like to get to the hotel before all the rooms are booked for the night."

"If you are staying over in town," the widow said. "Then I'll expect you for dinner promptly at six o'clock."

He smiled. "As long as you make your famous dumplings with one of those hens, you won't be able to pry me away from your table!"

She smiled like always, leaving him wondering if she'd heard a word he'd said, but from what Henry had told him, she'd gotten better at reading lips while she listened as best she could, and he was satisfied with that.

"Chicken and dumplings, it is," she said.

She heard me!

He whistled as he went back to his buckboard to retrieve her delivery. His mouth watered as he thought of his favorite dish, and suddenly, he couldn't wait for dinner.

Silver City, Nevada

Sheriff Tucker clenched his jaw; how could that angelic woman be promised to a man like Beau Dalton?

There had to be some sort of mistake.

It had been a long night with Beau hovering around waiting with him to see if the woman he prayed was Charlotte would wake so they could get to the bottom of this dilemma.

"I think we should go through her things to see if there is anything that could prove who she is," Beau finally said.

Sheriff Tucker stood at the window of the doctor's office staring out at the morning sun as it made its way up the boardwalk. He whipped his head around at the scraping noise behind him. He rushed to rescue the woman's trunks from Beau's clutches before he had a chance to open them.

He put a hand on the larger trunk to stop him.

"You don't have any right to go through her things; leave it be."

"I do if she's my mail order bride," he retorted.

"Since we don't know that yet, I'm the only one who has the authority to look in her things— but *only* if the young lady gives me permission."

"I'm not going to wait all day for her to wake up!" Beau said, grabbing for the valise.

Sheriff Tucker drew his gun. "Up until now, I've put up with your presence here, but at the point where you start disturbing the peace, it's time for you to go."

Beau's men rose from their chairs, guns drawn and trained on the sheriff.

"Tell your men to stand down," the sheriff yelled.

The doctor came barreling out of the exam room shushing them. "Keep your voices down; the young woman is awake."

Virginia City, Nevada

Rooster sat in the barber's chair, a hot towel wrapped around his face. He leaned back and closed his eyes and listened to the men gossiping. Ed and Jasper, two old miners who always hung out in the barber shop, sat in the corner playing a game of checkers.

"You should have come into town a little sooner," Jasper said to Rooster. "We had a couple of young ladies come here yesterday; one of 'em is stayin' at the widow's boarding house; the other one went to Silver City this morning. Had to meet her brother—or was it an uncle?"

"Either way, I suspect you'll meet the other one when you go back to Silver City, but you don't want to miss either of 'em," Ed said. "Pretty as can be—both of 'em. And they're about your

132

age, too. Maybe it's time you thought about gettin' hitched."

"You'll meet the one who stayed in town when you go to supper at the widow's place tonight," Jasper said.

Rooster sat up and lifted the towel from his whiskers. "How do you know I'm going to dinner there tonight?"

"Because you always take supper with her when you're in town, and b'sides, that woman feeds every stray cat that comes into town. Either way, you'll be eatin' her chicken and dumplin's t'night while the rest of us poor old widowers go hungry."

Rooster chuckled. "I doubt you're going hungry, but if you did, it's your own fault. Either one of you men would be a welcome suitor for the widow, and then you'd have all the chicken and dumplings you could possibly eat."

Jasper guffawed. "I ain't getting' hitched again for no chicken and dumplings; not when I can git 'em free once a month on Sunday after church at the community supper."

"Suit yourself!" Rooster said. He laid back in the chair and put the warm towel back on his whiskers; he wanted to look his best tonight.

For some strange reason, he was now looking forward to having dinner with the widow more than he usually did. Before, the cooking brought him in, but now he was interested in her house guest who seemed to be the talk of the town already.

Jasper took his turn, jumping Ed's last three checkers then rose from his chair, his old bones crackling. He moseyed over to the barber chair and put a hand on Rooster's towel. "I think we're just about ready to shave you," he said, grabbing the soap mug and bristled brush. He swished the brush around getting up good lather and then removed the towel from Rooster's face and began to lather him up. Then he took the straight razor, grabbed the bottom of the leather strap hanging from the side of the chair and began to sharpen it. When he was satisfied it was sharp enough, he began to go to work at trimming Rooster's stubble.

After Jasper finished shaving him, he wiped the excess shaving soap from his chin and set the chair upright. "I suspect you'll want to smell nice to go calling at the Widow Colton's house tonight," he said, holding up a couple of bottles of aftershave. "I've got lilac water and bay rum; on the house, take your pick."

Rooster took the bottle of lilac water, unscrewed the metal cap and sniffed. He made a face and pushed the bottle back toward Jasper. "I don't want to wear flower water; I'll smell like a girl. Let me smell the bay rum."

He took the bottle and waved it under his nose as he breathed it in. He smiled. "This is the one; it's woodsy, spicy, and manly. Now, how about that trim? My hair is just a mite too long."

When he was through, he tossed the barber two bits and left the barbershop while the older gentleman whistled and hooted over his clean appearance. His next stop would be at Jake's tailor shop at the end of the boardwalk, where he knew his friend would loan him a suit of clothes for the evening.

Rooster stood on the porch of the Widow Colton's boarding house, pulling at the knot in his tie that suddenly felt as if it was choking him as he knocked lightly on the door. He could hear the woman humming through the house as she neared the front door. His mouth watered as the aroma of chicken and dumplings drifted out through the screen enclosure. His stomach growled. He'd gone without his lunch to make room for the dinner he'd looked forward to all day.

The widow greeted him with a smile and stepped aside, inviting him in. "If you'd like to help me carry the heavy stuff in from the kitchen, I'll slip you an extra piece of pie."

She winked at him and he chuckled. She was such a good woman, he couldn't understand why none of the older widowers hadn't seen her worth before now.

"I think I'll have to take you up on that offer," he said as he followed her into the kitchen.

He balanced the platter with the baked chicken in one hand and the large tureen full of dumplings and gravy in the other, and followed the widow to the dining room. At the far end of the large table sat a very beautiful young woman. She glanced up at him with wide blue eyes after he set the food in the center of the table without spilling a drop. She dropped her gaze and pushed a stray, reddish-blonde curl behind her ear.

"Mr. Fick," the widow said, getting his name wrong—as always.

Rooster didn't have the heart to correct her—especially not in front of her house-guest. Maybe if the opportunity presented itself, he'd find a way to work it into conversation with the beautiful young woman.

"I'm Darla," she said, offering her hand, and he rounded the table, taking full advantage of the chance to touch her porcelain skin—just to see if it was as soft as it appeared from across the room. He confirmed it was as he grabbed hold and pressed the back of her hand to his lips and kissed it gently.

From behind him, the widow cleared her throat, causing Darla to jump and snatch her hand from Rooster's grasp.

"I'm very pleased to make your acquaintance, Mr. Fick," she said with downcast eyes, her cheeks blazing with a dark pink that contrasted against her milky skin.

Rooster cringed. Caught between being a proper gentleman and wanting to correct the widow without coming across as rude and lacking in manners, he let it go and smiled. "I'm pleased to be dining with two such beautiful young ladies," he said, causing a giggle to erupt from both women.

"If I didn't know you better, Mr. Fick, I'd swear you were trying to get the whole apple pie to yourself tonight," the widow said.

He chuckled as he pulled out the chair at the head of the table for the older woman. "If I'd known it was apple, I might have tried harder."

The widow bowed her head and outstretched her hands to her guests at either side of her, Darla's hand reaching across the table for Rooster's. He slid his hand in hers, the warmth of it heating his arm all the way to his elbow. She rolled her hand in his and intertwined her fingers with his, making him wish the widow's prayer would go on for ages—just so he could keep hold of the delicate hand that fit his like a well-worn glove.

Shame filled him after he heard the widow say *Amen,* and he hoped the Lord would forgive him for being lost in the clutches of one of his angelic creatures.

"Amen," he said as Darla's hand slipped from his.

He paused for a moment, the warmth of her hand lingering on his. Stealing a glance at her from across the table, her full lips were turned up into a smile so bright her blue eyes almost twinkled like one of the stars at night out on the lonesome, dusty trail. He'd spent many hours staring up at the night sky while out on cattle drives and wondered about those stars—now, he had one close enough to touch.

"Eat!" the widow barked at him playfully.

Her voice startled him out of his reverie, but the spell hadn't broken between him and Miss Darla across the table. He forced himself to grab for the chicken gravy and dumplings even though he no longer felt hungry for anything except Darla's hand in his.

He rose from his chair when the widow held out the carving knife and fork for him to carve up the bird and serve it. He kept his eyes on the chicken, fearing if he dared look at Darla he'd accidentally lop off one of his fingers and bleed all over their meal.

He took a deep breath and served up the meat with a precision of manners even his ma would be proud of. He returned to his chair and fumbled with his fork and knife, trying to remember the rest of his ma's lesson on table manners. The last thing he wanted was for Darla to see him as a sloppy cowhand who didn't know how to use a fork. He'd grown used to eating with his hands out on the trail, meat in one hand and slopping up his beans with his bread. This had to be different or he would frighten the poor girl into thinking he was uncivilized.

"Tell us, Mr. Fick," the widow said around a bite of chicken. "How is it that you've come to be in the city before the weekend? Did your mean ole boss let you off work for the day?"

Rooster smiled. "You happen to be looking at a free man!" he said. "I'm my own *boss* now. I worked hard this past year and managed to earn myself a little spot of land in Nevada territory and it just so happens to have a silver mine on it."

He couldn't help but notice Darla's eyes widen at the mention of the mine. Her refined dress and mannerisms told him she was a woman used to the better things in life—things that cost money. Though she didn't act the part of a spoiled

Daddy's-girl, her soft hands had likely never washed a dirty dish or gutted and de-feathered a bird, or any other domestic chore the way the widow's calloused hands had.

"If I know that low-down, cheating rascal, Mr. Dalton, he probably made out better than you did with that deal," the widow said.

Rooster hadn't missed the stricken expression on Darla's face or the little gasp that made her jump at the mention of Beau Dalton's name. Did she know him?

"Where are you from, Miss Darla, and what brings you here to Virginia City?" Rooster asked, boldly changing the subject over to her.

He had a feeling he wasn't going to like her answer, but better to get it over with fast—like yanking out a piece of barbed wire from your finger the first time you string fence. He learned then that it was better to get to the blood and guts of it than to linger over something and let if fester.

"I've run away from home, actually," she said, a delightful smile curving the corners of her lips.

That's it? That can't be all there is to that story!

She cleared her throat, her cheeks turning pink; it became clear she'd gotten caught with the proverbial canary in her mouth.

"My father was forcing a marriage upon me with a man who is twice my age," she said, barely above a whisper.

Was she trying to defend her actions, or did fathers still do that sort of thing?

He paused, looking up at the Widow Colton and tried to imagine how he would feel if his pa had tried to force him into marrying her. She was a lovely woman, and an excellent cook, but that wasn't enough for him to want to marry her. Why, she was older than his own ma.

He shuddered.

"That would be enough to make me run too!" he said without thinking.

Both women smiled, but he detected a strain there.

"I'm here to start a new life," Darla finished.

His heart sped up; this was his chance— unless there was more to that story than she was letting on. Too often, with women, there was usually quite a lot more than they portray.

"There's a dance at the hotel tonight," he said. "Would you allow me to escort both of you lovely ladies?"

His question had been pointed more toward Darla, but the widow answered for them.

"I knew there was another reason to your being here on a Friday night! We'd be delighted if you'd escort us, wouldn't we, Miss Darla?"

Darla nodded and smiled, lifting her eyes to meet Rooster's once more before she busied herself finishing the last of the chicken on her plate.

ELEVEN

Virginia City, Nevada

Rooster hitched the widow's horse to her buggy. Though the hotel was only down the block, she was an older woman and needed to be driven. Darla, he assumed, was accustomed to arriving formally anywhere she went. If it were up to him, he'd have walked proudly down the boardwalk with Darla on his arm, the moonlight guiding their way.

He snapped out of his daydream and hopped up in the carriage to pull it around in front of the boarding house to escort the women. He was getting ahead of himself and caught up in feelings for a woman he only just met. He'd never escorted a woman to a dance before, and he'd certainly never kissed one the way most of the men his age had.

The very thought of kissing Darla sent tingles right down to his toes. He cinched the bow of his tie, making sure it was loose enough around his neck that it wouldn't cut off his air. He needed all the room to breathe he could get right now; his heart raced as he caught sight of Darla waiting on the front porch for him—alone.

"Where's the widow?" he asked.

She smiled, a feather from her hat fluttering in the breeze alongside the strawberry blonde curls to either side of her cheeks. "While you were out back hitching up the horse to the carriage, a man named—uh—Jasper, pulled up in front of the house and offered to escort her. Naturally, she accepted his invitation."

"Naturally!" Rooster said, chuckling.

That sly old dog; he took my advice after all.

He offered his arm to assist her down the steps of the porch. She tucked one hand in the crook of his elbow, the other grabbed the skirting of her light blue dress that matched her eyes, and held up the hem.

At the carriage, he paused.

It's the same as helping Charlotte. I have to hold her waist, he reminded himself, as he put a hand at Dara's waistline and assisted her up into the carriage like a gentleman would. He was certain she was used to that sort of treatment, and he certainly would try his best to accommodate her.

Rooster climbed up onto the seat of the carriage, careful not to sit on the skirting of her dress, but she pulled it toward her to allow him room. Once she settled in, her thigh was touching his but she dropped the flounce of her dress, draping it over his leg. If this was what it was like

147

to escort a lady to a dance on a Friday evening, he'd be happy to stay in Virginia City and court this woman if she'd have him.

Darla felt giddy as the handsome gentleman sat so closely to her in the carriage. She could feel the heat of his leg next to hers, and it sent shivers of excitement straight to her toes—the same way it had when he'd taken her hand at dinner before the widow had said a blessing over the food.

She felt foolish for having blurted out her circumstance in front of the handsome man, but she was desperate to let him know she was not a taken woman—not yet, anyway. Though she'd accepted the contract for marriage from Mr. Dalton, she'd made note of the unsavory talk about him during supper. Had she been wrong about Beau Dalton? Had he deceived her in some way? If he misrepresented himself, would she still be bound to the contract with him?

There had been no more romance in Beau's letters than she'd pretended when she'd talked about them to Charlotte. Here she was in the most romantic setting a woman could ask for— complete with a handsome escort, and she was stuck in a contract of marriage with another man. Could she possibly stay in Virginia City and take a job—perhaps at the boarding house, where she was more than aware of the widow's need for such help? If she did, would Mr. Fick come calling?

He drove the buggy slowly toward the end of town where music from a violin played a slow waltz. She glanced up at her escort, suddenly regretting the contract she'd entered with Mr. Dalton. If she never showed up in Silver City, would the seemingly ill-tempered Mr. Dalton come looking for her? Her conscience told her she needed to honor the contract, but her heart told her to run from it and see where things might take her with her handsome escort instead. One dance with this handsome man wouldn't be considered a betrayal, would it? Though if Beau could look into her soul and pluck out her feelings right now, she imagined he would consider her thoughts a definite betrayal of their contract.

How was she to know she'd meet someone else *first?*

He pulled the buggy up to the hotel and she put a hand on his to stop him; she suddenly wasn't up to dancing in a crowded room, fearful the emotions she wore on her sleeve would show.

He stepped down from the carriage and reached for her, assisting her down from the seat. She paused, his arms still around her; would she permit him if he tried to kiss her?

He cleared his throat and put a proper distance between them. "Would you care to take a walk along the boardwalk before we go in to the dance? It seems a shame to waste a night like this; the moon is nearly full, and the stars aren't usually this bright in town."

She smiled, her heart aflutter, as she tucked her arm in the crook of his elbow. "It's as if you read my mind, Mr. Fick. I'd like very much to take a walk in the cool, evening air."

They strolled along, and she found herself wondering about his given name; would he see her as a brazen woman if she asked to drop the formalities between them? She imagined he must have a strong name that matched his character, and admittedly, she was almost too curious to wait for him to offer. But wait, she must. He probably already had a preconceived notion about her, given the fact she'd admitted to running away from her father's home. She'd traveled a long way unescorted, and he might find that information to be quite brazen enough for one evening.

By the time they'd walked down one side of the street, he turned around before they reached the rowdy saloons and walked her back toward the hotel where the musicians played a familiar waltz that she'd heard many times at dances back in San Francisco. She wanted nothing more than to dance with this handsome gentleman, to be in his arms and feel his masculinity holding her captive—even if only for one dance.

But they couldn't; they were in the public street. What would the townsfolk say about her if she allowed herself to be wooed by this man? Would she suffer reprimand from the Widow Colton?

He bowed slightly. "If the lady would rather, a dance in the moonlight might be much more pleasant than being in that stuffy hotel fighting for space on the dance floor."

He'd read her mind again, or perhaps, it was her hesitation to join the others that made him advance toward her. With nothing more than a simple look from her, he pulled her close and placed a hand in hers, the other at her waist. He twirled her around in a slow waltz, and being in his arms was just as she'd imagined it only a moment before. His arms were strong and sure, his posture perfect, but if the average onlooker were to observe the scandalous space between them, they might suffer reprimand, but giddiness rushed through her at every twist and turn in his arms. Would she feel this way when Mr. Beau Dalton held her in his arms? How could she possible love two men at once?

Did she *love* Mr. Fick?

Perhaps not yet, but there was certainly something stirring in the air between them this lovely evening. She tried so hard to remember her commitment with Mr. Dalton, but her head was dizzy, and her heart beat only for this man in her arms.

How could she ever love another man?

All she wanted was this man—for his arms to remain around her and his lips to touch hers.

Rooster couldn't ignore the gentle sighs from Darla any longer. If he didn't kiss her he would regret it for the rest of his life. She'd given him all the signs; the leaning into his frame, the little whiny sighs, and the fluttering of her lashes. He'd seen enough women swoon over a fella, and Darla had all the symptoms.

He leaned in and they both paused as if frozen in time; he wanted to kiss her—needed to kiss her, their faces so close, their lips almost touching. Her warm breath tickled his mouth, making him salivate with a desire that could only be quenched with one taste of her lips.

"Mr. Fick…" she whispered, but her voice trailed off as her lashes fluttered once more.

How long would he keep allowing her to call him by the wrong name? Would this refined lady find his country name too uncouth for her liking? She was probably used to men with more sophisticated names than Rooster, but he *had* to tell her and get it over with. He imagined it rolling off the end of her tongue like a yard-bird she would no sooner pluck than to dress it and cook it. Probably best to see how a woman like Darla reacts to it instead of keeping things so formal.

Rooster ignored his inner dialogue that tried to warn him to be upfront with her as he closed the space between them and pressed his lips gently against hers.

"Mr. Fick," she whispered again.

He cleared his throat; it was now or never.

"My name is not *Fick,*" he said.

She blinked and gasped, breaking the spell between them. "I'm promised to another man—in Silver City," she blurted out. "I believe you know him; his name is Beau Dalton."

So much for telling her my name!

TWELVE

Silver City, Nevada

Sheriff Tucker held up a hand to Beau and his men. "Whoa!"

Beau took an aggressive step toward the sheriff. "You don't give me commands like I'm some sort of pack horse. I've waited all day to talk to her and now I'm going in there to see my bride and you aren't going to stop me!"

The doctor came from the exam room, shotgun in his hand and aimed at Beau and his men. "No one but the sheriff is going in there to talk to her, so he can question her," the doc said, raising the gun from their bellies to their faces. "I don't want *any* of you men as patients, but don't press your luck with me; I'll use this if I have to in order to protect that young lady from you brutes upsetting her."

Sheriff Tucker walked around Beau and past the doctor, confident that the man could take care of himself. He'd had his fair share of forced surgeries in his career, with outlaws expecting him to remove bullets at gun-point. The doc finally got smart and decided to protect himself, and the sheriff couldn't fault him for that.

Beau threw his hands up and cocked his head toward his men. "Let's go!" he barked to them, and then whipped his head back around to face the sheriff. "I'll be back tomorrow, and I expect to collect my bride then—and not you or any shotgun is going to stop me."

They let the door slam behind them, and after they left, the doc collapsed into the nearest chair and rested the butt of his gun on the floor beside him. "I thought for sure I was going to have to make a patient out of one them, and I don't like making my own business. I prefer to let it come to me."

"Thanks, Doc," Sheriff Tucker said. "For having my back with them; are you sure you don't want the deputy job?"

The doctor shook his head and wiped the sweat from his brow. "I have enough to worry about just keeping myself and the townsfolk alive!"

The sheriff smirked at the doc's comment.

"You and me both!"

He paused before entering the room where the young woman rested. "How is she?" he asked. "Did she tell you her name yet?"

Doc shook his head. "Honestly, she looks familiar to me, but I can't place her."

Sheriff Tucker reached up and turned up the wick in the sconce on the wall; the room had grown dark and the extra light exposed the worry lines on the doctor's face.

"Would you say," the sheriff asked, pausing for the right words to finish his sentence. "That she looks a little like Rooster Figg?"

The doctor snapped his fingers and jumped up from his chair, his lips pursed. He nodded. "I think you might have something there; but wasn't Rooster supposed to be sending for *her?*"

"It's possible she could have come looking for him," Sheriff said.

"I agree," Doc answered. "Anything is better than the possibility that pretty young thing promised herself unknowingly to Beau Dalton."

"If she did, I have no other choice but to hand her over to him," Sheriff Tucker said. He shivered at the thought of it; she was a beautiful woman and from the little bit of time he'd spent in her company, she was a sweet woman—much too good for Beau.

"Let's go see if we can get her to remember," Doc said. It'd be a shame to have to let her go to such a man. Isn't there a way around that? Doesn't the poor thing have a choice? I

159

mean, especially if she didn't know what kind of man he was when she agreed to marry him."

The sheriff blew out a breath and shifted his feet, folding his arms across his chest. He couldn't think past the shudder that rocked him at the image of Beau kissing that poor girl. He was not a gentle man, and a woman like her needed the patience and love of a gentleman—something Beau was not.

That man had been a thorn in the side of most of the men in town in the two years since he'd bought his spread just outside of town. He'd managed to turn a mean profit from the land and he constantly threatened to start a range war over petty things—most of those troubles originating with him and his men. They were always up to something, and always one step ahead of the sheriff, and with both feet just barely inside the lines of the law. He knew his boundaries well—as if he had someone in his pocket. Whoever that someone was, had kept him well-informed— enough to turn a profit at the expense of the other ranchers and without any means of defense for the shady dealings.

"Let's worry about that if it becomes an issue," Sheriff Tucker said. "We've got enough trouble on our hands just having her here without borrowing more trouble than we can handle."

He opened the door to the dimly-lit room, and the nurse excused herself.

The room smelled of antiseptic and candlewax, but he could still detect the flowery aroma of the young woman; it was a scent that would stay with him even if she couldn't be his. He'd likely yearn for her even after Beau took her away, but he prayed he wouldn't have to surrender her to him.

She looked up at him with a serious expression as he moved deeper into the room.

"I don't know if you remember me or not, but I'm Sheriff Tucker, and I found you wandering along the trail between here and Virginia City." He searched her expression, wondering how a woman like her could fall prey to a man like Beau. "I'd like to ask you a few questions, if I may."

She nodded, her green eyes a little hesitant.

"We're all sort of *eager* to know who you are and what brought you to Silver City,"

She sat up on the cot where she'd been resting, her wavy, auburn hair unpinned and draped over her shoulders.

She turned up her nose just a little bit—enough that Sheriff Tucker thought it was cute.

"I'm afraid I'm not able to tell you why I'm here or what brought me here, exactly," she said barely above a whisper. "But I feel as if my heart belongs in Silver City for some reason—if that makes sense."

Probably not to rest of the world, but to him, yes. He nodded and smiled. "If it's any consolation, my heart belongs in Silver City, too."

She smiled, but a far-off look still captured her striking green eyes—eyes that almost mirrored Rooster's, though his did not interest him the way this woman's eyes did—except that they were similar. Although her eyes were a deeper green, they were very much alike—too much alike to ignore.

He wanted to blurt it out and ask outright if she was Charlotte, but experience warned him to be gentle with someone after they'd suffered a head injury like hers. It was always best to let the person come to their own conclusion in their own time—no matter how much he wanted to confirm that Beau's accusations of the woman were not true. But until she confirmed it wasn't the truth, he had to leave it open in his mind as a possibility.

"Are you able to tell me your name, Miss?"

He was almost afraid of her answer.

She looked at him blankly, tears welling up in her eyes, her lower lip quivering. She shook her head slowly.

"You have a gentleman who has been waiting to see you," the sheriff said with hesitation. "He believes your name is Darla Wingate. His name is Beau Dalton. Does any of that sound familiar to you."

She paused and then wiped at a tear on her cheek. "Both names sound very familiar to me—yet foreign at the same time, if that makes any sense."

Sheriff Tucker felt the hole in his heart for this woman growing wider. He was beside himself with worry that she was promised to Beau—but why? Had he really been so taken with her that his heart should break if she married another man? How could he love her when she didn't even know who she was? If she didn't know, it stood to reason that he didn't know either. He guessed it was more of a feeling he had about her than anything else. He'd had plenty of offers to court young women over the years, but hadn't felt that special spark—until he met this woman. For that reason alone, he *had* to know who she was.

"Is it possible there is something in your trunks that could tell us both who you are?" he was almost afraid to ask. He wanted so much to ask her outright if her name was Charlotte; he wanted to ask her about saying Rooster's name just before she'd passed out in his arms, but the doctor had warned him not to prompt an identity out of her. He'd claimed that if ideas were put in her head before she remembered on her own she might latch onto it and then be disappointed when it didn't come to pass. If it were up to him, he'd ask her and get this over with before Beau came back to claim her.

Her eyes widened making them even more lovely.

"You have my trunks and my valise?" she asked.

The sheriff smiled. "You remembered your things; that's a good start. With your permission, I'll bring them in the room and you can go through them."

She nodded, the faintest hint of a smile curving her full lips.

Sheriff Tucker rose from the chair and went into the lobby of the doctor's office to retrieve her things. Doctor Goodwin was there at his desk with the lamp low, his round, wire-rimmed spectacles low on his nose. He dipped his pen in the inkwell and scraped across the journal page with precise strokes he was certain only the doctor himself could read. The sheriff assumed he was journaling the young woman's progress from the look of it. He didn't disturb him, and the doc never looked up from his notes. It was just as well; the sheriff was in no mood for small talk. His nerves about the young woman made him shake. Why was he so nervous to discover her identity? Probably because his heart was already vested in hers and he wasn't ready to let her go to another man.

He knew it was foolish to think such things about a woman he didn't even know, but he was a firm believer in *love at first sight*. It had been what had brought his own ma and pa together; his pa had proposed to his ma only an hour after they'd met, and they've enjoyed thirty blissful years together. He'd already grown affections for this woman through Rooster's stories of her.

Stacking the valise on top of the smaller trunk, he hoisted it up onto his shoulder and carried it in the room where the young woman waited for him. She smiled nervously when he set it down in front of her. He quickly left the room to get the other trunk, returning with it and set it down with the other luggage.

"If you're not ready to look in your things, we can wait till morning," Sheriff Tucker said.

She shook her head, her auburn hair swishing over her shoulders. He wanted so much to twist one of those curls around his fingers and draw her lips to his. He sat in the chair across from her, too aware of the flowery scent of her hair. It drew him to her with a force that could only be recognized as love.

Lord, please don't let her identity crush my heart.

She slowly opened the valise, rifled through the contents with a confused look about her, before she finally pulled out a stack of letters tied with a yellow, silk ribbon. She held them, staring at them until she looked up at the sheriff, her green eyes full of question and concern.

"They're from Beau Dalton and addressed to Miss Darla Wingate of San Francisco," she whispered.

I guess that answers my question; the possibility of her being Charlotte is not looking too good.

THIRTEEN

Virginia City, Nevada

Rooster immediately put distance between himself and Darla. His hands shook, and his lips stung, his heart breaking into a million fast-thumping pieces. How could she allow him to kiss her if she was promised to another? Worse, how could a woman like her promise herself to a man like Beau Dalton?

"I'm sorry," she whispered. "I should have told you, but I couldn't help myself—I was so drawn to you that for a moment, I felt I was falling *in love* with you."

Too many questions cluttered his mind, and her admission did not help matters. He felt the love for her too—as if it had been real between them. How could he deny that? More than that, how could he fix this? If he told Darla the truth about Beau, would she believe him, or would she think he was selfishly trying to persuade her against the man she was promised to? On the other hand, if he didn't warn her about the kind of man Beau was, he would never forgive himself for letting her walk into what must be a trap of lies. How could he possibly turn her over to a man as evil as Beau Dalton?

There was only one solution to this problem. He knelt on one knee, pulled Darla's hand into his and looked up into her dreamy blue eyes that glowed in the moonlight. "Will you marry me, Miss Darla Wingate?"

A slow waltz emanated from the hotel, but the silence of her hesitation drowned it out. "How can I marry you, Sir, when I don't even know your name?"

He rose from bended knee, removed his Stetson, holding it in front of him against his chest. "Allow me to introduce myself formally," he said. "My name is Rooster Figg."

She drew a hand toward her mouth to cover the giggle that escaped her lips.

Rooster fumed.

So much for telling her my name!

Silver City, Nevada

Sheriff Tucker felt his throat constrict. "Are those *your* letters, Miss?" he asked the young woman he'd rescued out on the trail. "Are you Miss Darla Wingate?"

She looked up from them, tears welling in her eyes. "I don't know; I don't remember corresponding with anyone, but they must be mine—they're in my valise. Darla is a familiar

171

name to me, but I'm not sure it belongs to me—it seems sort of strange on my tongue."

"This Beau Dalton claims the two of you have a marriage contract; is there one in your bag—perhaps with the letters?"

She rifled through the bag once more and pulled out an envelope that was separate from the others and held it out to him. "You look at it—I'm afraid," she whispered.

"What are you afraid of?"

He took the envelope and their fingers touched. They both froze, the warmth of her touch lingering on his was almost enough to take his breath away. She gasped and looked up at him, her green eyes softened,

"I'm afraid of being forced to marry a complete stranger," she said. "If that is a contract, you're going to have to get me out of it. I'm not the sort of woman who would marry someone she's never met!"

Sheriff Tucker had to admit he was happy to hear such a thing from the young woman, but he had no idea how he would get her out of the legally binding contract. Others had tried over the years, but it usually involved a lengthy series of hearings in front of the judge.

He opened the envelope and pulled out a paper. There was no doubt that it was a marriage contract, but it was only one half of it. If Beau had the other half to this contract with her signature on it, then it was legal, and she would be hard-pressed to get out of it. It was only a matter of time before Beau would come to claim her and they didn't have time to schedule a hearing in front of the judge in Virginia City.

"Do you remember signing a marriage contract?" He asked.

An idea sparked in him and he knew it was a long-shot, but he had to try for his sake and for hers. He jumped up from the chair and went out to the lobby where the doctor still sat at his desk.

"I need to borrow your pen and a piece of paper," he said to the doctor.

Dr. Goodwin stopped what he was doing and gave the sheriff the things he asked for. No sooner did the sheriff have them in hand, than he ran back into the room with beautiful young woman he prayed was not Darla Wingate.

He placed the piece of paper in front of her and handed her the quill pen. "Put your signature on this page"

She looked up at him and frowned. "You want me to sign Darla's name?"

He chuckled. "You say that like you're not Darla."

She shrugged "I suppose I am—I mean, I have to be, don't I? Those are my things—at least the luggage is mine, I think. I wish I knew for sure."

He tapped the paper in front of her. "Put your signature on this page and then we'll know for sure."

She began to scribble a signature and then grabbed the letters tied with the yellow silk ribbon, looking back and forth between the name on the letter and the page she was signing.

She giggled nervously. "You would think if this was my name I would know how to spell it!"

Virginia City, Nevada

Rooster took a step back, putting distance between himself and Darla once again. He clenched his jaw, his heart breaking all over again.

Was she laughing at him?

"Can I ask what's so funny?" He asked.

"You're Rooster Figg!" she said with a giggle.

Rooster sighed heavily. "I do believe that is what I just said," he said, impatience in his tone. "But I don't see what's so funny about my name."

"It's not your name I'm laughing about. Charlotte told me all about you," she blurted out. "And here I am with you dancing with you and kissing you and accepting a proposal from you!"

175

Rooster felt the blood drain from his face. "How do you know Charlotte? Do you mean my sister, Charlotte?"

She nodded and giggled. "We met each other on the train from San Francisco, and we traveled together until we got here. I became overheated on the stagecoach and she stayed an extra day to nurse me back to health."

Rooster chuckled. "I can't believe she's here in Nevada! Are we talking about the same girl?" He held up his hand in front of him, chest height. "Short, scrawny little thing, about so tall? Reddish-brown curly hair and green eyes?"

Darla giggled and nodded vigorously, grasping his arms with both her hands. "Yes! She's a delightful girl and we became very fast friends."

"Where is she now?"

"She left for Silver City yesterday morning just after dawn. She rented the carriage from the livery."

Rooster thought about it for a moment. He left Silver City right about the same time; how had he not run into her along the way? Then he remembered his stopover at the Colton farm and relaxed.

"I need to send a telegram first thing in the morning to make sure my friend, Riley Tucker—he's the sheriff—watches out for her until I can get home. I'd hate for her to run into Beau Dalton."

Darla's countenance changed. "Beau Dalton isn't the kind man, is he?" she asked.

How could he put it to her as delicately as possible without making her feel like a fool?

"What exactly was it that he told you about himself?" Rooster asked.

"He told me that he was a young and successful rancher, and a God-fearing man."

Rooster bit his bottom lip to suppress a smile, but he just couldn't hold in the chuckle no matter how hard he tried. "Beau Dalton is certainly a wealthy rancher, but I wouldn't call him successful by any means—not the means by which he gains his wealth, and he's old enough to be your father," he said. "You don't have to take my word for it; you'll be able to see that with your own eyes. As for his temperament, Beau Dalton is anything but God-fearing. He's not a kind man. My personal dealings with him are that he's a swindler, a liar, and a dangerous man."

Darla smiled and raised an eyebrow. "In that case, I'm glad I've accepted your proposal instead of his."

Rooster stopped; the wording of questions about Charlotte had taken over in the forefront of his mind, and it suddenly dawned on him that he'd missed something.

"Wait a minute," he said. "Did you just say you accepted my proposal?"

"Yes!" she squealed. "I said it once before, but I think you missed it. I will marry you, Rooster Figg—that is, if I can get out of that contract with Beau Dalton."

Rooster scooped Darla up in his arms and twirled her around whooping and showering her with kisses.

"Don't you worry, Miss Darla; my friend, Sheriff Tucker will get you out of that marriage contract with Beau Dalton."

He twirled her around the street, dancing to the fast waltz echoing out from the hotel.

FOURTEEN

Silver City, Nevada

Charlotte paced the length of the exam room at the doctor's office, willing her mind to cooperate with her. She didn't believe she was Darla Wingate any more than the sheriff had, but she couldn't prove otherwise. They'd looked all through her trunks and found her dresses and personal things that were all familiar to her—even a wedding dress she knew belonged to her ma, but none of the items in the valise had been familiar—

least of all, the letters of correspondence with Beau Dalton.

There had to be another explanation; was it possible she could have picked up another woman's valise on the train?

The train!

She'd come from the Barbary Coast—that was something she hadn't remembered until just now! She continued to pace—what else could she remember if she really put her mind to it?

From the other side of the door, she could hear the low voices of the doctor and the sheriff. Were they talking about her? The sheriff had promised to protect her from Beau Dalton, claiming that he was a dangerous man and not to be trusted. There would be no convincing the man she wasn't his bride if he found out about the letters she had in her possession.

What had she gotten herself into?

If only she could remember what had brought her to Silver City in the first place. Was she running toward something or away from someone or something?

I wouldn't travel on my own, so who did I travel with? Darla Wingate? Who is she, and where is she?

She wore a path in the floor, nearly making herself dizzy pacing in such a small space, but she just couldn't sit still. She had to get out of here—had to get out and see what it was or who it was she'd come to the city for. The feeling deep in her gut told her that her heart belonged in Silver City—but for who? Surely not for a man like Beau Dalton. She was smarter than that. She would never get herself mixed up with someone who would deceive her like that. Her pa had brought her up to question everything—to never let her guard down.

Pa...

If only she could remember more than that. Would her pa have let her go off alone and travel such a great distance on her own? She had to have been traveling with Darla—but why?

She opened the door and walked out into the lobby where the sheriff and doctor were huddled over his desk and discussing something quietly. When she crept into the room, the wood floor squeaked, giving away her presence.

The sheriff rushed to her side. "You shouldn't be up. You need your rest," his voice was strong and authoritative, and she thought it very sweet of him to worry about her. Was it *him* she was here for, and she just couldn't remember him? Surely, she would remember such a handsome man—especially if she'd ever kissed him Would his lips be as soft as rose petals against hers?

"I'm fine," she said. "I don't need to rest; I need to figure out who I am, so I can keep from having to marry Beau Dalton, and I think Darla could be in trouble."

The sheriff raised an eyebrow over his deep blue eyes. "What makes you think she's in trouble?"

She focused on the man who towered over her by at least a foot, his shoulders broad and strong, his face kind. A day's scruff peppered his jaw and she thought it made him look rugged—handsome. Her lashes fluttered at his closeness, her heart doing the same.

"Did you remember something?" the sheriff asked, bringing her out of her reverie.

She nodded. "I think I must have traveled with Darla from the Barbary Coast because my pa would never let me travel alone—he would have…" her voice trailed off and she focused on Sheriff Tucker's badge. She reached out and placed a hand on it and closed her eyes against tears that came uncontrollably.

Sheriff Tucker instinctively drew her close; he couldn't help himself. Her tiny frame fit comfortably in his arms, and he allowed her to sob.

"What's wrong, Darlin'?" he asked, kissing the top of her head.

"My pa—he was a deputy—your badge made me think of him—but it also made me remember he's dead!"

Sheriff Tucker walked down the boardwalk to the telegraph office, the early morning sun heating up the street. Though most of the town was still closed up, the General Store was open, and Willy was already stacking his father's wares out in front of his store. The sheriff knew Charlie would have his window open at the telegraph office—the old man's business was always the first one open in the morning and the last to close down at the end of the day.

He walked toward the end of the boardwalk, glancing up casually to make sure Beau and his men were not still in the area. If he could get a telegram to Virginia City, the livery owner might be able to tell him more about the carriage she rented. But more than that, she had to have come in on the stage, and surely the Overland Express office would have record of her travel.

The young woman had not been satisfied with the letters she found in her valise, claiming they were familiar to her, but didn't feel they were hers. Was it even possible her things could have been mixed up with another's? It was too far-fetched to even think about, but as long as she refused to believe it, he would do everything he could to prove it wrong. She admitted to knowing the name, Darla, but didn't believe it was *her* name.

If Rooster was in town, he'd send him to Virginia City and forget the telegrams altogether, but then again, if he was here, perhaps the mystery of the young woman's identity would already be solved.

With Rooster gone off somewhere, there was no one else here that he trusted enough to be discreet about the telegrams. The other merchants in town were good men, but they also liked to spin a yarn, and he feared any news that would come would end up in Beau's hands before it ended up in his.

He wished he had more answers, but after the young woman had suffered a breakdown about her pa's death last night, the doctor had given her something to help her sleep; after that, she'd been no good for getting information out of her. Poor thing had relived her pa's death as though she was just finding out for the first time, but she remembered it had been more than a year ago—about the same time Rooster had arrived in Silver City. He knew that Rooster had also lost his pa just before he'd come to Nevada Territory, but that alone wasn't proof the young woman could be his sister, Charlotte. He did have to admit the evidence was stacking in his favor that she was Charlotte. If only the doc was wrong about asking her questions that would lead to real answers, but the last thing he wanted to do was to hinder her natural recovery.

Lord, help me to protect her from Beau Dalton, and help her remember who she is before it's too late.

He stepped up to the telegraph window. "Hey, Charlie," he said. "I need to send a telegram to Virginia City."

The old man pursed his lips, white whiskers peppering his weather-worn face. "I'm afraid it'd be faster to walk it there," the old man said, his words whistling between the large gap where he was missing two teeth on the bottom. "The lines are down—have been since yesterday."

The sheriff sighed. "Is anyone working on them?"

Charlie nodded. "It might take 'em a week or it could only be an hour—no way of tellin'. Sorry, Sheriff. Do you need a pony rider?"

Sheriff Tucker shook his head. The only pony-rider in town had just signed on to do Beau's bidding. He supposed he couldn't blame the young lad. There was more money in working for Beau than the occasional work he got from the other folks in town.

He walked back to the doctor's office, loud voices prompting him to hurry inside. When he opened the door, Beau's men trained their guns on him again. He drew his hands up and stepped into the office slowly.

"You'll hang for sure if you shoot a man of the law—there won't be any questions about it," the sheriff said, putting his back to the wall.

The foreman laughed. "That's if they catch us!"

Sheriff Tucker narrowed his eyes. "Oh, you can bet you'll get caught; I've just sent off a telegram to the U.S. Marshall, so you better just move along."

He knew it was a lie, but he had to do something to diffuse the situation before it got further out of control.

"It'll take him nigh two hours to get here," Beau said, smiling wide and showing off his tobacco-stained teeth. "By that time, I'll be long gone with my bride you're holding here."

"She isn't your bride," Sheriff Tucker said. "Her name is Charlotte Figg, and she's Rooster's sister."

Another lie—but he prayed not.

"Now that's where you're mistaken, Sheriff," Beau said, his gun trained on him. "You see, before you got here, we got the Doc here to admit she found my letters in her valise."

The doctor flashed Sheriff Tucker a look of remorse. "I also told you she's resting and shouldn't be moved before she's fully recovered from her head injury."

"I hate to inform you, Beau," Sheriff said. "But you can't marry her until she's of sound mind. It ain't legal if she doesn't know who she is."

"I've got proof," Beau barked at him. "She has my letters in her possession, and I don't need her to be of sound mind; all I need is those letters and the contract."

Sheriff Tucker remembered her signature just then. "Let me see your contract with her signature on it."

Beau handed it to him and he walked over to the doc's desk where he'd left the signature page and compared the two. He held them up and showed Beau. "I had her sign this last night, and she couldn't even spell the last name without checking the name on the envelopes you claim belong to her, and look—the signatures don't match."

Beau snatched the page from the sheriff's hand and held it up in comparison to his contract. "That don't mean nothing! She could have faked the signature—to get out of having to marry me because the two of you are putting ideas in her head."

"You can't legally take her with you until she's well enough and she admits she's Darla Wingate—and she still wants to marry you," the sheriff said. "That, and I already told you, I have good reason to believe she's Charlotte Figg."

He knew he was no match for Beau and his guns, and they'd already broken the law by holding him and the doctor at gun-point, but he was willing to let that go if the man would see reason to let the young woman come to her own conclusions about who she was.

"I don't care who she is," Beau said. I aim to marry that pretty little gal, and neither of you are going to stop me!"

"Don't do anything foolish or you'll be answering to the Marshall when he gets here," the sheriff said.

"I paid good money to have her brought here, and I aim to get my money's worth."

Sheriff Tucker didn't have the money to pay him back or he'd offer it; he'd given almost his last dollar to Rooster, so he could bring Charlotte from the Barbary Coast—even though she's already here right under his nose in the Doc's office—and he can't do anything about it! The guards had come from the territorial prison and taken the prisoner, but they'd brought a bank draft made out to Rooster, so he didn't have the money yet, but he'd have it as soon as Rooster came back from Virginia City.

"Let me buy out the contract you have with her!" Sheriff Tucker blurted out.

Beau looked at him and threw his head back, a mean sort of laughter spewing from his mouth. "Sheriff, there ain't enough money in the whole territory to buy me out of marrying that sweet little woman."

A ruckus in the center of town drew their attention away from the situation in front of them. "Go see what's going on out there," Beau said to his foreman.

No sooner did he open the door when one of the townspeople rushed up to the door with a whoop and a holler. "Did you hear? Old Buford hit a large vein of silver out at his mine. He's struck it rich!"

Beau flashed his men a look. "His mine is adjacent to the one that no-account Rooster Figg just *stole* from my safe a few nights ago, isn't it?"

"Yeah," both his men said, winking at Beau.

"That's not true," Sheriff Tucker said. "Rooster worked an entire year for free for that mine—after you swindled it out from under him once already!"

"You find that Rooster Figg and arrest him," Beau said. "I aim to get that mine back from him. I'll get my money's worth from it—or I'll take it out on his sister you got holding up here. That pretty little woman is going to marry me one way or another—or Rooster Figg is gonna hang for stealing from me—with or without a trial, and you won't stop me, Sheriff."

FIFTEEN

Virginia City, Nevada

Rooster sat in a chair in the office of Will Curee, a lawyer who was the preacher's son and a mutual friend of his and the sheriff's, hope filling him for the first time in a long time.

"So, what you're saying, Will, is that if Darla is already married to someone else—to me, then Beau Dalton can't force her to marry him?" he asked.

"He could contest your marriage, but it would take so long and cost him so much money that in the end, the judge would rule in your favor because you'd probably be married nigh a year by then, and most likely have a little Rooster on the way!"

Rooster chuckled. "The last thing I would ever do would be to name my son after myself. Don't get me wrong now, I wear the name proud—now that I'm an adult b'cause my pa gave me that name, and it's not that I don't appreciate my pa's sense of humor when it came to naming his only son. But even he admitted he should have thought it through a little more once I started school and the teasing began. But by then it was too late to do anything about it and it hasn't been easy growing up with the name."

"Kids can be cruel," the lawyer said. "I went to school with Sheriff Tucker and those kids teased him something fierce because he liked wearing his hair long then, and they'd tease him and tell him he needed to put on a dress. One of them even brought his ma's parasol to school and threw it at him, but those same kids grew up and most are merchants in Silver City now—and they respect him."

Rooster chuckled again. "I'll have to remember to ask him about that."

"Just be nice or he's liable to tease you right back," the lawyer said.

Rooster cleared his throat. "He's already done that—so I owe him one!"

"Well then in that case," he said. "You have my blessing to tease him."

They both laughed.

"If you'd like me to," Will said. "I'd be more than happy to file some papers with the court here, so we can get a jump on this thing with Beau Dalton. I can file a complaint against him for misrepresenting himself to her. His letters clearly state he's twenty-something, and we both know that man is well into his forties. I can also add that she signed the contract under duress because she was afraid her own father would force her into an equally unsuitable marriage if she didn't agree to

Beau's requirement that she sign the contract before he would provide traveling monies to come here. I'm sure if I put my mind to it, I can think of a dozen other things to add to it. But I'll need the letters if this goes to court."

Rooster nodded. "She claims that my sister, Charlotte, took her valise to Silver City with her by mistake and the letters are in there. Once she learned what kind of man Beau was, she was really upset that she'd done such a foolish thing, but if you assure me that we won't be breaking any laws by marrying, then we'll go on ahead to Silver City and get married."

Will cleared his throat. "If it were up to me, you'd be married here—before you go back. If she's still unmarried when you both go to Silver City, Beau could collect on his contract immediately, and there wouldn't be any protection for her—other than the sheriff stepping in on her behalf for safety reasons, but Beau could easily overpower him with that contract."

"But who is going to marry us here and now?" Rooster asked. "It's after hours now, and the Justice of the Peace is surely gone for the day, and your pa is in Silver City."

"Not many people know this about me, but I am an ordained minister—my father made sure of that. He told me the only way he was going to pay for law school for me was if I could marry more couples than I had to divorce."

Rooster laughed. "That's funny, actually, and I agree with him wholeheartedly."

Will laughed. "Yes, I suppose it is a bit ironic, but certainly in our favor."

"How soon can you perform the ceremony?"

"I can do it in about an hour—after I go home for dinner," he said. "If I know Ellie, she'll have my hide if I don't let her help your bride get ready for her wedding—that, and if I'm late for dinner, I'll be sleeping in the barn with my horse tonight."

Rooster laughed. "I'll let Darla know and we'll be back here in an hour."

He walked out of the office feeling like the luckiest man in Nevada Territory. Not only was his sister here to visit with him, but he was about to marry a woman his ma would be proud to call a daughter-in-law if she was still with them.

Ma and Pa, if you're looking down from Heaven, protect Charlotte until I get back to Sliver City, and bless my marriage to Darla.

Darla welcomed Ellie Curee into the room where the Widow Colton sat with her while she got ready for her wedding. The older woman stitched one of twos blue garters to put around her thighs to hold up her stockings—they were to symbolize her *something blue* and her *something new*.

Ellie handed her a hankie with a little blue flower on it. "I brought this one just in case you needed something *borrowed* and *blue*."

Both women giggled and hugged. "It was so kind of you to think of me," Darla said.

"For my *something old,* I have the lace hem and the pearl buttons from my mother's wedding dress. I'm afraid there wasn't much left after the moths found a hole in the steamer trunk where she'd stored it. She'd had a new dress made by a dressmaker for the wedding to Mr. Von Barron— the wedding I ran out on to come here."

Darla paused for a moment. She'd run out on two weddings now; would the women think she was fickle because of it? It was tough enough for her not to believe it of herself, even though both occasions were necessary, in her opinion. She would never run out on Rooster, though. He was a good man, and everything Charlotte had told her about him was true—and more.

Would it be wrong or even bad luck for her to wear a wedding dress that was intended for two others before Rooster? Bile rose in her throat. She couldn't do this—not like this.

She stood abruptly. "I can't do this!" she squealed.

"What's wrong?" the widow asked, shock in her eyes.

Darla picked up the folds of the expensive dress and then flounced it to the floor. "I can't wear this dress. It was made for my wedding to Mr. Von Barron, and then I was going to wear it for my wedding to Mr. Dalton. I can't start my marriage off on the wrong foot—I mean—with the wrong dress."

Ellie smiled. "I wasn't sure if you had a dress, so I brought mine! It's in the carriage."

She ran out to get the dress and the widow sat next to her and began to brush her hair. "Mr. Colton wasn't the man I was supposed to marry either. My father had me promised to a snooty fellow after sending me to a finishing school. He never liked my Henry Colton; his father was a farmer and used to bring us milk and his mother brought us eggs. When Henry and I eloped, my father disowned me for the first couple of years we were married, but I wouldn't have traded even one minute with my Henry to gain my father's approval. You follow your heart and don't worry about your father's promise to marry you off to Mr. Von Barron, and don't worry about breaking your promise to Mr. Dalton because he is a vile man. You follow your heart; Mr. Fick is a good man."

Darla giggled. "Did you know his name is *Figg?*"

The widow chuckled. "Of course, I know, but as long as he's worried about correcting me about his last name, he won't pester me about using his given name. Don't ever tell him this, because if you do, I'll deny it, but I can't call him by *Rooster* because I'm too afraid I'll laugh when I say it and I don't want to hurt his feelings. He's too good of a man for that."

Darla turned around and hugged the elderly woman. "I promise it will be our little secret."

Darla stood in front of the young Reverend Curee in her borrowed dress. All that mattered to her now was marrying the right man, and that man was Rooster Figg. She imagined her father bursting through the door of the boarding house and forbidding her to marry him when the reverend asked if there was anyone present who should not agree that they be wed. Her heart raced at the very thought of it, and at the same time, she wished that her parents could be there to give their blessing. Perhaps after some time had passed she would take Rooster home with her to meet her parents, but until then, she was content to leave her childish ways behind and cling to her husband as a grown woman.

"Do you, Rooster Figg, take this Darla Wingate to be your lawfully wedded wife, to have and to hold from this day forward, in sickness and health, for richer or for poorer, till death parts you?" The preacher asked.

Rooster winked at Darla and smiled. "I do, I certainly do! I'm going to love you for the rest of my life, Miss Darla!"

Darla giggled and lowered her head shyly, her cheeks feeling warm.

"And do you, Miss Darla Wingate, take Rooster Figg to be your lawfully wedded husband, to love and obey, in sickness and in health, for richer or for poorer, till death parts you?"

She smiled and winked back. "I certainly do too," she said. "And I'm going to love you, Rooster Figg, for the rest of my life!"

"Do you have a ring?" The preacher asked.

Rooster pulled a small pouch with the drawstring from the pocket of his rented suit jacket and pulled out a ring. Darla leaned in and looked at it, a little gasp escaping her lips.

"Where did you get that ring?" She whispered.

"I had Mr. Rudgar make an exception for me and open the bank vault to retrieve it. It belonged to my ma."

Darla's breath hitched, and tears welled up in her eyes. "I'm honored that you would trust me with such a treasure."

He slipped it on her finger, her hand a little shaky.

"With this ring, I thee wed."

"By the power vested in me by the territory of Nevada, I now pronounce you man and wife. Rooster, kiss your bride!"

Low laughter erupted in the room by the few onlookers, but a hush followed as soon as Rooster pulled Darla into his arms. She sucked in a breath until his lips touched hers. He swept them across hers slowly at first, and then deepened the kiss with a vigor of hunger she quickly became lost in. The rest of the room went away; only Rooster and his soft lips remained, kissing her and sending tingles of delight all the way to her toes.

SIXTEEN

Silver City, Nevada

"Why did Darla ever agree to marry that Beau Dalton?" Charlotte asked. "He's meaner than a rattlesnake!"

Sheriff Tucker cocked his head to the side and raised an eyebrow. "Did you hear what we were saying out here?" he asked.

"There was so much shouting, it was hard *not* to hear—but I'm glad I did hear it—or else I wouldn't know that I'm really Charlotte."

Sheriff Tucker's eyes grew wide and he rushed to her side, pulling her into his arms and laughing madly.

"I'm so glad you remember," he said. "I made Rooster a promise I'd protect you once you came to Silver City, and here you are—and I've already failed you!"

He let her slip from his arms and threw his hands up, and then folded them over his broad chest. "I'm sorry, Charlotte, for not protecting you like I promised, but I'm so glad you remember who you are—that's what counts here."

"I didn't say all that!" she said, offering him a smile. "And if this *brother* of mine ever shows up, I'll let him know you've done all you can to protect me, but all that shouting gave me an idea, if you're willing to listen."

Sheriff Tucker stood there, arms folded and frowning—it was kind of cute—in a *manly,* tough-guy sort of way. "You mean, you're *not* Charlotte?"

She smiled and shrugged. "I don't exactly know for sure, but it seems logical."

"So, what's this great plan you have?" he asked.

"I figure that we can maybe fool Beau Dalton into thinking I'm *really* this Charlotte, and then I can get out of having to marry him," she said. "If you were so convinced, maybe he will be too."

"I appreciate your trying to help with this, but I think the only way that plan is going to work is if you can come up with the real Darla Wingate," he said. "In the meantime, I think it would be best to *hide* you while Beau is preoccupied with the silver mine. I'm also going to send a telegram to my friend, Will. He's a lawyer in Virginia City, and I'm going to have him file some papers to put a stop to what Beau is trying to do."

"Where do you plan on *hiding* me?" she asked.

"The only place I can keep an eye on you," he said. "At my place—above the jail."

Charlotte shook her head. "No!" she said. "What kind of woman do you think I am? I'm not staying with a man I'm not married to!"

Sheriff Tucker smiled. "Then, I suppose you'll have to marry me—for the sake of *propriety*."

"I'm not sure if I'm insulted by that, but I bet I am; that sounds like a marriage of *convenience,"* she said, turning up her nose. "Besides, I told my ma I'd never marry a sheriff!"

Truth-be-told, she was mighty attracted to him, and could see herself making him coffee in the morning, and cuddling with him by the fire, or looking out at the stars on a moonlit night. They would have two kids—a boy and a girl, and they would both have curly hair and blue eyes like their pa.

Whoa! She was getting way ahead of herself. That badge on his chest made him both appealing and repulsive at the same time. She liked the idea of having a sheriff to protect her, but she didn't want to worry about him every night like her ma had worried about her pa.

"I can always turn you over to Beau Dalton and you can marry him—though he doesn't wear a tin badge, he does stand on the other side of the law most of the time."

"No!" she squealed. "He's old enough to be my pa, and not in a good way—in a scandalous way."

"Well, which is it?" Sheriff Tucker asked. "Are you willing to take your chances with Beau or will you marry me—for safety *and* propriety?"

"When you put it that way it sounds very unappealing. Do I have any other choice?"

"Not really. Besides, I promised your brother that I was going to marry you when you came into town, and at least this way, I'll be able to uphold one promise."

She scrunched up her face. "Why would you promise that? What if you didn't like me once you met me? You're as bad as Darla—agreeing to marry a complete stranger. How can you marry me when you don't even know my name?"

"For the sake of fooling Beau, we're going to convince him you're Charlotte Figg, so that's the name you'll use when we go in front of the preacher—that is, just as soon as you agree."

She turned her back to him and took a deep breath.

"I know it isn't going to be a *real* marriage, but a girl likes to be *officially* asked, you know."

He touched her arm, getting her attention, and then bent down on one knee, taking her hand in his.

Charlotte let a gasp escape her lips; she couldn't help it.

He was *really* proposing!

She gazed into his soft, blue eyes that sparkled as if they contained real love—for her. It was absurd to dream such a thing, but if she allowed herself to admit it, she felt the same way right now. It was silly, she knew, and it was only a marriage of convenience—for her safety, but that didn't mean she wouldn't take it just as seriously as he was.

He kissed the back of her hand, his lips lingering, sending shivers all the way to her elbow. Why did his touch affect her in such a way—a way that made her want to be in his arms and have his lips touching hers?

He gazed up at her with dreamy eyes. "Charlotte Figg, will you do me the honor of being my wife, my soulmate, and my best friend? Say you'll marry me and make me the happiest man alive!"

Tears welled up in her eyes, putting a lump in her throat. "Yes! That is…if I'd really make you the happiest man alive."

He nodded and his lashes fluttered. "You will; I really believe you will."

She sensed a hesitation in him—as if he wanted to seal the deal with a kiss, but was a little too shy, and she liked that. If she wasn't mistaken, he was smitten with her. He had that same dreamy look in his eyes the woman on the train had when she described her letters of correspondence!

"She's a mail order bride!" she blurted out. "The woman on the train; I met her on the way here. It was just a flash of a memory, but it wasn't a memory of me. It was a memory of seeing her—sitting across from me, and I remember her being very *chatty*. She seemed nervous—about marrying her intended."

"I would be too if I was about to marry someone as mean as Beau Dalton," the sheriff said.

"I wish I could remember more," Charlotte said. "But it comes to me in bits and pieces—as if I'm seeing it all happen in front of me all over again."

"Keep telling yourself that you're Charlotte, so that when the preacher says the name it won't be foreign to you. I've got some arrangements to make, such as sending telegrams and getting the license from the Justice of the Peace; you get yourself ready, and I'll bring the preacher here back to the doc's office, if that's alright. The church is in Virginia City."

Sheriff Tucker ran back down to the telegraph window. "Please tell me," he said, trying to catch his breath. "That the lines are back up."

Charlie smiled, showing his missing teeth. "I tell you, Sheriff, it's like a miracle!"

"Send a telegram off to Virginia City and tell them we need the Marshall here just as soon as he can get here, and send another one to Rooster— he's either at the hotel or at the Widow Colton's boarding house. Tell him to get back here immediately."

He prayed his friend would understand if he didn't wait for him to get back to town before marrying his sister—that is, if she was indeed Charlotte. The woman's safety was his utmost concern, and he was certain Rooster would give his blessing. He'd practically given it to him already, even though he couldn't be certain the man had taken him seriously.

Either way, he was jumping in with both feet and marrying a woman he only just met—an angel who took his breath away every time he was near her. He could easily love her for the rest of his life, and he didn't fear that she wouldn't do the same for him. He'd seen the way she looked at him when he'd proposed, and there was certainly the makings of love in her eyes.

Charlotte unfolded her ma's wedding dress and laid it across the cot in the doctor's exam room. Her heart beat as if butterflies were fluttering around in her ribcage, but it was a happy sort of nervousness. She was marrying a handsome sheriff and his kindness and concern for her made her feel at ease. But was it right to marry a man when she didn't even know who she was?

She closed her eyes, fingering the lacy fabric of her ma's gown, trying to remember anything about the woman. She was about to put on her dress; was it right to wear it if it didn't belong to her? She was certain it belonged to her own ma, but she just couldn't remember her the way she wanted to—the way a woman should think and feel when putting on her ma's wedding dress and marrying in it.

Sadness filled her as she twirled the ribbon sash around her fingers. She wished her ma could be here to help her get ready—wished her pa could give her away on her wedding day. Surely, if she married the sheriff, it would be until death parted them. She didn't believe in divorce—she believed in happily-ever-after; did Sheriff Riley Tucker believe the same thing?

She slipped the dress over her head and it was a perfect fit. A knock at the door startled her and she wiped the tear from her cheek before answering.

The nurse entered the room and immediately smiled. "You look lovely, dear," the woman said. "I know I could never take the place of your ma at a time like this, but would you like me to button the back of the dress for you?"

Charlotte nodded and forced a smile.

"It's your wedding day, sweetie," she said, lifting her chin. "You should make your ma proud by being happy; you won't find a finer man in this town than our sheriff."

She was right, and it felt good to hear that the sheriff was so revered.

"He'll be a good husband to you, and if you really are Charlotte Figg, he's your brother's best friend, so you know Rooster approves of him."

That was also good to know; if only she could remember this *Rooster*. What kind of a name was that anyway? Was it a nickname? You'd think she would remember such a name, but something was blocking it and that frightened her.

"Doctor Goodwin carried over a full-length mirror from the dress-maker next door, if you'd like to see how you look in your momma's dress."

"Would you mind helping me with my hair first?" Charlotte asked.

She sat in a chair and handed the nurse her bone-handled brush. It wasn't silver like Darla's. She gasped.

"What's wrong?" the nurse asked.

"I had another memory of Darla," she whispered.

"Was it a memory that was your own, or was it a memory of seeing Darla do something?"

"She was in bed—ill for some reason," Charlotte said. "I was handing her a silver-handled hairbrush. I watched her brush out her long hair; it's a reddish-blonde color. I suppose you would call that strawberry-blonde."

"Do you know where she is now?" the nurse asked her.

"No," she whispered. "But I believe it was only a few days ago. She was going to meet me here when the doctor told her she was well enough to travel in the heat."

"We do know one thing for certain," the nurse reminded her. "The real Darla is expected here to marry Beau Dalton."

"That poor, innocent girl has no idea what she's gotten herself into," Charlotte said. "I wish there was a way to warn her to keep her from having to marry Beau Dalton."

"Other than being married already, I can't think of anything, but I imagine that's what the sheriff is up to right now," the nurse said. "He's sending telegrams all over the territory asking the sheriff in each town if they have seen her. The sooner he can find her, the sooner he can help her."

"That's smart thinking," Charlotte admitted. "I'd hate for her to show up here and have Beau snatch her as soon as she arrived."

"Don't you worry another minute about it," she said. This is your wedding day, and this whole town is on the lookout for Miss Darla Wingate."

Charlotte blew out a breath. "That does make me feel better."

"Good," she said as she put the last of the pins in Charlotte's hair. "Let's go get you married to that handsome sheriff!"

She stood and picked up the bottom of the dress; her ma had been a little taller than she is, and she didn't want to let the dress drag on the floor, fearful it would snag on a splinter on one of the wood floor planks.

In the lobby, in the corner, just as promised, the doctor had brought in a full-length mirror. She inched toward it shyly until she stood before it. She was almost too afraid to look.

Lifting her gaze, her heart beating like the hooves of a team of horses running at full speed, she admired the lacey folds of the skirting. She turned around slightly to view the bustle. She admired her reddish-brown hair pinned back in a perfect chignon and the little spiral curls to each side of her face. Peering into her green eyes, there was a familiarity there. It wasn't that she'd forgotten what she looked like, but it was as if she was looking at someone else in the reflection.

She twisted her hands together to calm them, turning her head to the side to look at the dress once more. The tiny pearly buttons down the back of the dress were all fastened, the satin sash was tied over the bustle into a perfect bow, and the fluted lace along the wrists fluttered like the wings of a butterfly when she moved her arms.

Her vision blurred, and her mind took her back for just a flicker to a time when she was young, and giggles came easy for her. She pushed at the sleeves of her ma's wedding dress over her tiny hands, her arms swimming in the folds. The hem of the dress lay in clumps on the floor over a set of tiny feet. She looked up at her ma, the woman giggling and fussing over her.

"Someday, I'm going to marry a sheriff just like pa," she'd said to her ma.

Her breath hitched.

"I'm Charlotte Figg!"

SEVENTEEN

Charlotte waited for her cue and then walked out into the lobby of the doctor's office with her hand tucked in the doc's elbow. Since her pa wasn't able be there to give her away, he'd offered, and it had touched her heart so much it'd brought tears to her eyes.

She walked toward her groom, her gaze trained on him; he would be her focus for the rest of her life, and she would vow to make him the happiest man alive—just like he'd declared. She would do everything her ma had taught her by example of how to be a good wife and eventually a ma—she hoped, anyway. The fact that she knew who she was made this day an even better occasion, and it had made her want to marry him even more. She knew she no longer *needed* to marry him, and for that reason alone, she would honor the promise she'd made to make him the happiest man alive. He had a kindness in his eyes—like her pa's, and she didn't fear an uncertain or unhappy life with him because of it. They had their whole lives to get to know each other, but the way she felt today, was as if she'd known him all her life. It seemed that every step she'd taken had led up to these steps she now took toward him—the man she would love for the rest of her life.

Sheriff Tucker watched his bride walk toward him and he felt like the luckiest man in all of Nevada Territory. Not only was she beautiful, she remembered she was Charlotte, and she still wanted to marry him even though it was no longer an absolute necessity. She'd made a good point that, although she'd regained her memory, it wasn't proof of her identity—at least not as far as Beau would be concerned. There was still the matter of the letters she couldn't explain how they'd come to be in her possession. He could see in her eyes that she believed it could all be explained away, and perhaps she'd used it as a means to secure the marriage. She hadn't needed to, and he'd played along, knowing the whole time he would have been sad had they decided not to marry after all. He aimed to prove his commitment to her for the rest of his days on this earth.

He loved her already; he wouldn't have asked for her hand if he hadn't, and he aimed to prove that to her if necessary. But he had a feeling he wouldn't have to; she already knew how he felt about her. He could see it in her eyes as she walked toward him now.

His heart raced as she continued toward him, wearing a smile so wide it probably matched his own. Lord help him, he already loved her—the same way his pa must have felt when he'd been so spontaneous as to propose to his ma mere hours after they'd met. He got it now, but if anyone would have asked him even two days ago if he believed in love at first sight, he would have laughed in their faces.

Charlotte stood next to her groom, her hand in his; her fingers tingled all the way to her elbow as his fingers wrapped around hers. Their hands were a perfect fit—just like her parent's hands. Her ma always told her that if she could find a man whose hand fit hers like a well-worn pair of gloves she should marry him and never let him go. Her ma had been full of a lot of sentiment when it came to her pa. Their love was like none other she'd ever known, and she prayed her life with Sheriff Riley Tucker would mirror that of the wonderful life her parents had together—minus the early deaths, of course.

She would not think about death today; it was a day of rebirth and a day to be celebrated because life was too short not to.

The senior Reverend Curee placed his hand over the couple's hands. "Dearly beloved, we are gathered here today in the sight of God to witness the coming together of these two people into holy matrimony. In as much as these two have consented to become one flesh by the joining of hands and hearts, what God has joined together, let no man put asunder. If there be anyone present who believes these two should not be joined together, let him speak now or forever hold his peace."

The door to the doctor's office flung open.

"Not without my blessing!"

Charlotte jumped, but when she looked into the man's familiar green eyes, the eyes she'd last seen in a young boy who'd left her side after their pa's burial, she couldn't help but let loose a good pig-squeal. He'd grown into a man since he'd been gone, but she would know him anywhere.

"Rooster!" she cried.

He rushed to her and pulled her into his arms. "Did you think I'd let my baby sister get married without me here?"

Behind him, a young woman entered the office, a shyness about her that Charlotte recognized.

"Darla, how did you get here?" Charlotte asked.

"I came here with my husband," she said with a shy smile.

Charlotte sucked in her breath. "Your husband!"

Rooster gave her a squeeze. "Me, silly girl. I married her!"

Her hand flew to her chest. "How? What about the other…uh…?"

"Beau Dalton?" Rooster asked. "We filed papers in Virginia City to get her out of the marriage contract, and the lawyer suggested we get married before we came back here; I hope you aren't upset with me for not waiting for you, Charlotte."

Sheriff Tucker stepped forward. "As long as you aren't upset with me for not waiting either."

The two men shook hands, and Darla rushed to Charlotte's waiting arms. "We're sisters!" they said in unison.

"You have my blessing," Rooster told the sheriff. "Don't let me interrupt; carry on. I believe the preacher was about to finish this and announce the two of you. But is it alright if I give the bride away?"

Charlotte let go of Darla and hugged her brother once more. "Of course, it is."

He gazed happily into her eyes, tears misting them. "I know Ma and Pa are looking down from Heaven today, and they're proud of both their young'uns. You made a good choice; he had my blessing before you even got here."

"What are you talking about?" Charlotte asked, giggling nervously.

"He told me about a week ago—and several other times, that he was going to marry you when you got here," Rooster said.

She scoffed. "I already knew that; he told me."

"Well, I told him he needed to ask you; he *did* ask you, didn't he?"

Charlotte smiled. "Yes, he did."

Rooster bent down to kiss his sister on the cheek, and then motioned for Sheriff Tucker to take her hand so they could continue the ceremony.

Reverend Curee cleared his throat and lifted his gaze, doting on everyone in the room with his eyes. "Who gives this woman to be wed today?" he asked.

"I do!" Rooster said, his chest puffed out and a smile as wide as the entire Nevada Territory.

He kissed his sister on the cheek and smiled. "I love you, Charlotte, and I'm proud of you."

She smiled, tears welling up in her eyes. "I love you too, Rooster. Thank you for being here with me."

He stepped out of the way and stood on the other side of Sheriff Tucker.

"Riley Tucker, do you take Charlotte Figg to be your lawfully wedded wife, to love and to cherish, in sickness and in health, for richer or for poorer, for as long as you both shall live?"

Sheriff Tucker looked at his bride and smiled. "I do!"

The senior Reverend Curee turned.

"Charlotte Figg, do you take Riley Tucker to be your lawfully wedded husband, to love and obey, in sickness and in health, for richer or for poorer, for as long as you both shall live?"

Charlotte squeezed her soon-to-be-husband's hand and smiled, a single tear rolling down her warm cheek.

She nodded. "I do!"

He pulled a simple ring from his pocket and showed her the engraving inside the gold band.

I love you forever, "My pa had it engraved for my ma for their twenty-fifth wedding anniversary."

"It was my ma's ring, and before that, it was my grandma's; is that alright?"

Charlotte smiled, another tear slipping down her cheek. "Yes," she said, nodding vigorously.

He held up her hand and slipped his ma's wedding band over her ring finger without any effort. "With this ring, I thee wed." He raised her hand to his lips and kissed the back. "It's a perfect fit," he said. "I knew it would be."

She fanned her fingers in front of her for just a moment to admire the ring that bound her to two generations before her. It was a good feeling to belong to a bigger family.

The preacher cleared his throat. "You may kiss your bride, Sheriff."

Charlotte lifted her gaze to meet her six-foot-tall, sheriff-husband's blue eyes, his brown curly hair touching his ears just below the band of his Stetson. He leaned in and she sensed a hint of musky manhood mixed with woodsy aftershave; it made her lashes flutter. Her lips parted, her breath shallow as his lips captured hers. Warm and soft, his mouth swept over hers, his warm breath tickling her with the scent of peppermint leaves. With one arm wrapped around her narrow waist, his other hand at the nape of her neck, he drew her face closer, deepening the kiss. She was nearly limp in his arms, helplessly smitten with him, and falling deeply in love.

EIGHTEEN

Sheriff Tucker held Charlotte close, trying his best to keep his emotions decent. He wanted to make her his wife as much as he needed his next breath, but he'd vowed to protect her, and until the Marshall arrived, he'd have to stay on guard and keep his boots on—for the time-being!

"You get some sleep, Darlin'," he said, kissing the top of her head. He knew better than to let his lips find hers or he'd never leave; he'd take her straight to his bed and love her the way a man loves his newly-wed woman.

Rooster and Darla, were due there any minute. They'd been fortunate enough to spend their honeymoon night in Virginia City, but a union between the sheriff and his bride would have to wait. "I don't like this any more than you do, Darlin'," he said.

"Then bolt the door, ready the shotgun and stay here," she practically begged him. "I don't like the idea of spending my wedding night hold up in this room with Darla instead of my husband!"

He buried his face in her neck, breathing her in like she was a little piece of Heaven that had fallen from the sky. "You know I wish I could; I don't like this any more than you do, but your brother and I have to keep the two of you and this town safe until the Marshall gets here with a little backup. It's my job to uphold the law in this town—and to keep you and everyone else in this town safe. I'd rather spend my wedding night protecting you and knowing you're safe than to spend the rest of my life standing over your grave wishing I had."

She opened her mouth to plead with him but a knock at the door downstairs to the jailhouse stopped her.

"That's Rooster now. I'll send Miss Darla up to keep you company. I know it's not right, but for now, it'll have to do."

He kissed her full on the mouth with a sort of desperation that he wasn't sure if he'd ever see her again. "I love you; make sure you lock the bolt behind me" he said, and then he was gone—before she had a chance to argue with him.

"I love you too," she called after him, but all she heard was his boots pounding on the wooden steps as he ran down to the jail to meet her brother. She bolted the door and waited for Darla.

Sheriff Tucker opened the door, and immediately threw his hands in the air. Beau stood behind Rooster, pushing a revolver into his ribs, alternately moving it around him and training it on the sheriff. His foreman had one arm wrapped around Darla's waist, the other clamped over her mouth. Tears rolled down her cheek and he could see she struggled to breathe around the fingers digging into her cheeks.

Beau waved the gun at him. "Drop your gun-belt and toss it over there," he said, motioning with his head.

Sheriff Tucker flashed Rooster a look as if to tell him to *play along* as he unbuckled his gun-belt slowly and tossed it behind him, knowing if he threw it over toward Beau, it would give the man too much advantage over him. At least with his gun behind him, he still had some chance of control over it.

"Let the lady go!" Sheriff Tucker barked at him. "Your fight is with me and my deputy."

Beau snickered. "You call this no-good claim-jumper a deputy? He ain't even wearin' a gun! But he's broken the law and I want him arrested!"

"He's not a claim-jumper, Beau," the sheriff said. "He earned that worthless mine."

Beau twisted up his face. "I'm not talking about the mine," he spat when he spoke. "I'm talking about this pretty little filly who belongs to me, and this law-breaker was trying to steal her away from me!"

Beau turned to Darla and ran the back of his hand down her cheek affectionately. She bucked and squealed, trying to break free, but Beau grabbed her arm and yanked her away from his foreman and snaked his arm around her waist, thrusting her into his side.

Sheriff Tucker looked between the two men, both with guns drawn, searching for an opportunity to get Darla out of harm's way and overpower the gunmen.

"I'm not marrying you," Darla whimpered.

Pipe down little lady; you're going to complicate this, and I'll never be able to rescue you.

Beau threw his head back and laughed, and then ran his tongue up the side of her face nice and slow. "Your marriage to the *chicken* ain't legal; you signed a contract with *me,* and that makes you my wife—not his!"

She bucked again.

"You're a feisty one," Beau said, tightening his grip on her. "I like that."

Rooster whipped his head around and elbowed Beau in the gut; he buckled at the waist, his grip on Darla enough for her break free. Two of Beau's men entered the jailhouse, one of them smashing his empty whiskey bottle against the door-jam and held it out in front of him as a weapon, his drawn pistol in his other hand.

Sheriff Tucker didn't like these odds; four against two.

Darla bucked once more, trying to break free, and Rooster pushed her out of the way just long enough for his fist to connect with Beau's jaw.

Sheriff Tucker dove for his gun; the click of a hammer stopped him just short of it.

"Turn around nice and slow and back away from your gun, Sheriff," Beau said though gritted teeth. "And if you're lucky, I won't shoot you."

He was as good as dead either way, and so was Rooster; he had nothing more to lose. He grabbed for the gun and rolled over on his back, but the foreman kicked it out of his hand.

He pointed his pistol at the sheriff's head and pulled back the hammer.

"You got a death-wish, Sheriff?"

Sheriff Tucker watched Beau's foreman's twitchy trigger finger, waiting for him to pull the trigger, the gun aimed between his eyes. The slightest move, and he would roll to his side; a moving target was harder to hit. His pa had taught him that, but he'd never thought he'd have to put it into practice.

"Be careful, Sheriff; no fast moves," the foreman warned him. "Or I'll make your pretty, new wife a widow, and then she'll be mine!"

It wasn't long before Charlotte heard loud voices from downstairs, muffled between floors—but she detected a tone that suggested it wasn't her brother at the door, but rather, Beau and his men.

She dimmed the lantern and pulled down the window shade, searching the room for something she could use as a weapon.

The fireplace poker!

She grabbed it and stood on the other side of the locked door, her back to the wall and her breath coming out in short bursts mixed with inaudible whimpering. Her whole body shook. She blinked repeatedly in the dark room as if it would somehow manifest her protective husband.

More shouting.

She crossed her knees and rocked on her heels to keep her bladder from emptying.

"Lord, please keep my husband safe," she whispered into the darkness. "Don't let Mr. Dalton kill us."

She flinched at the loud voices; they were fighting.

Was that glass breaking?

"God, please save him," she cried out.

Two shots rent the air, but it was her own scream that startled her.

Warmth trickled down Charlotte's thighs, turning cold by the time it reached her ankles. Her breath held in, she listened, eyes wide.

Where was Rooster? Was he lying dead with her husband?

Footfalls on the stairs brought her back to reality. She raised the iron poker above her head and braced herself to fight to the death against the intruder. She bit her bottom lip to keep it from trembling and to stifle the cries that needed to escape.

The door bumped and her breath hitched; she hadn't meant to make a sound, hadn't meant to alert them that she was hiding.

Another bump against the door and it burst open. She jumped and tried to scream, but couldn't find her voice. Her face felt suddenly cold and clammy, and the room began to spin when the men entered the room and surrounded her one-by-one. She felt her limbs give way underneath her frame and the iron poker fell to the floor with a clang.

"Let's get her to the boss," one of them said.

She knew her thoughts were slipping from her and she tried her best to hang onto them, but it all went away when they placed the grain sack over her head.

Lord, please send help.

The man hoisted her over his shoulder and she was helpless to fight him as he carried her down the stairs and away from the only help she knew.

Sheriff Tucker groaned, his face smashed up against the cool, wooden floor of the jailhouse. His eyes focused on the steel bars only a few inches from his face. He could barely move without pain shooting from his shoulder to the tips of his fingers.

Beau had winged him.

Reaching up, he touched his shoulder and then brought his hand in front of his face. It was bloody, and his shoulder stung. He tried to wiggle the fingers at the end of his injured arm, but they were numb.

A faint memory of screaming reverberated in his ears.

Charlotte…

He'd been helpless to save her or Darla from being taken away by Beau and his men. It angered him to his very core; she was his bride, and if Beau hurt her in any way, he couldn't trust that he'd obey the law and show the man justice. He swallowed hard and reached his good hand toward the steel bars and gave them a good rattle.

Beau had locked him in his own jail.

Chapter

NINETEEN

Sheriff Tucker lifted his head to search for his hat. His pa, the sheriff before him, had given him only one piece of advice when he'd turned over the keys to him.

"Son, don't ask me how I know this, but do yourself a favor and tuck a spare key to the jail cell in the rim of your hat—in case you should ever get locked in your own jail—accidentally, of course. Most outlaws are quick to take away your

gun in haste, but rarely, if ever, do they take away a man's hat or his boots."

His hand went to his head, but it wasn't there; his heart drummed out a beat more than twice what it should be when he eyed his Stetson upside down in the hallway making him wish he'd chosen to put the key in his boot instead.

A groan from the adjoining cell caused him to whip his head around a little too fast. He'd lost a fair amount of blood judging by the stain on the floor where he'd been knocked out for the past few hours.

"Get up, Rooster," Sheriff Tucker called out to him, the pitch of his own voice making his head woozy. "I need you to get my hat for me, so we can get out of here and get the women back from Beau."

Rooster was slumped against the brick wall and turned his head just enough to face the bars; he looked out. "I can't reach that!" he complained, rubbing at the bloody mark above his eye. "I guess I should be thankful they didn't kill us, but I have a feeling we're only alive, so we can suffer whatever comes next."

The sheriff pointed at Rooster's head. "I think you're going to need to have Doc stitch that up. You're probably right about whatever is coming next. See if you can reach my hat."

"Why do you need your hat, Riley?"

He tore his shirt tail and twisted it to make a tourniquet for his arm. "Because there's a key in the rim; we kind of need it to get out of here."

"Why didn't you say so in the first place?"

Rooster scooted across the floor with the amount of energy of a schoolhouse full of kids and pushed his arm through the bars, stretching his fingers a far as he could but the hat was just out of his reach.

"Whad'ya suppose we do now?" he asked, pointing to the barred window above his head. "Wait until the sun comes up so the people in town can laugh at us when they let us out of here? Not to mention, that'll give Beau too much time to harm to our wives—if he hasn't already. How long have we been in here, anyway?"

He reached into his pocket to retrieve his pa's watch, but it wasn't there. "My pa's watch is gone!" he said, turning his pockets inside out. "The deed to the mine is gone too."

He gripped the bars of the jail cell and shook the door. "We need to get out of here, now!"

A noise came from the alley; Rooster's head snapped up. "You s'pose that's Burt?"

Sheriff Tucker shrugged and they both listened.

"Maybe he's not too drunk yet and he can help us."

The sheriff shook his head. "If he's trying to bed down in the alley, he's too drunk to help us!"

"Burt!" Rooster hollered, shaking the cell door to make it rattle. "Burt, the sheriff needs your help."

Something slammed into the back door, causing both men to jump.

Baa baa

"That's not Burt!" the sheriff said. "It's Millie Farmer's goat.

Another *baa* followed by a high-pitched bleat.

"Little Millie," Rooster said. "Come here, Little Millie."

Sheriff Tucker swatted the air in Rooster's direction. "Don't call that goat in here; she'll eat my hat, key and all, and then we'll be stuck in here"

Rooster blew out his breath with a whoosh.

"I didn't think about that."

The goat head-butted the door again and it swung open, the hinges squeaking.

Baa baa

Millie entered in through the hallway of the jailhouse; her milk sack so full, it had to uncomfortable for her. She stopped and dropped a few pellets on the floor midway toward them.

"I'm going to deputize you, Rooster, just so you can clean that up!"

He poked his finger into his chest. "Me? Why me?"

Sheriff Tucker scowled at him. "Because you called her in here!"

"I still think she can help," Rooster said. "What have we got to lose?"

"My hat and the key for starters!"

"Here Millie, get the sheriff's hat and bring it to me like a good little goat," Rooster said.

"No!" Sheriff Tucker said.

It was too late; Millie trotted forward and sucked up the hat into her mouth with her lips.

"Give it to me, Millie," the sheriff said in his most friendly tone. "Come here, girl. Give me my hat and I'll find you a real treat."

Rooster leaned up against the bars and watched the sheriff trying to coax the goat over to him, so she'd give up his Stetson and not eat it—key and all. He pulled a stick of beef jerky from his vest pocket and stuffed it between his teeth and bit off a piece and began to chew.

Sheriff Tucker shot him a glance and scowled. "How can you eat at a time like this? We have to figure a way out of here. In case you forgot, our wives are with Beau Dalton."

He bit off another small piece of the long strip and then stuffed the rest back in his pocket.

"You know I'm always hungry," he said in his defense. "Besides, I won't be any good for rescuing Darla if I'm weak and hungry."

"Give me the jerky, Rooster!"

"No!" he said, putting a hand over his pocket as if the sheriff could take it from him through the barrier between them. "Get your own!"

"It's not for me! It's for Millie!"

Rooster crossed his arms and scowled.

"You want me to give my beef jerky to that goat?"

Sheriff Tucker nodded. "Now you're catching on! It's an exchange for the hat—so we can get the key and save our wives from Beau."

He pulled the stick of jerky from his pocket and handed it to the sheriff. "Only for Charlotte and Darla."

The sheriff bent down at eye-level with Millie and offered the jerky through the bars of the cell door. "You bring me my hat and I'll give you the treat, just like I promised."

Rooster guffawed. "Do you think that goat understands you?"

"She understands tone of voice just like my horse; you treat an animal kindly and they understand."

"I'm not so sure that'll work on a bear," Rooster said, chuckling.

Sheriff Tucker ignored his friend; he'd never known him to act this way, but he supposed he was acting out to hide his worry about sister and Darla—if he had to guess.

"Here, Millie, come get the treat."

Millie dropped the hat and ran toward his outstretched hand with the jerky in it. Sheriff retracted his hands inside the bars before she could grab it.

"I don't think she understands your tone," Rooster said.

"Get my hat," the sheriff continued to coax with a patience not many would have. "And I'll give you the jerky."

Baa baa

"*Baa baa,*" Rooster said back to the goat.

Millie looked up at Rooster. *Baa baa*

"*Baa baa,*" Rooster repeated.

Sheriff Tucker shook his head. "You can't be serious right now," he whispered.

Millie went over to the sheriff's Stetson and picked it up with her teeth and nibbled on the corner a little, then trotted over to Rooster and dropped it on the floor right in front of the bars.

Rooster poked his arm through the bars and snatched up the hat. "I guess you just have to speak the right language!"

Sheriff Tucker shook his head and chuckled as he tossed the jerky out to the goat. "If I hadn't seen it with my own eyes I would have never believed it."

Rooster handed the sheriff his hat and he pulled at the stitching in the rim to retrieve the key. He drew it to his mouth and kissed it with a smack and then snaked his good arm around the bars and put the key in the lock. He stood in front of the cell where Rooster was still locked in.

"Let me out, Riley; why are you just standing there?"

"Do you, Rooster Figg, agree to abide by all the laws of the territory of Nevada, and uphold those laws?"

"What is this? Let me out of here!"

Sheriff Tucker shook his head. "Not until you answer the question."

"Why are you asking me that?"

"I'm deputizing you!"

Rooster shook his head. "No, you're not!"

"It's the only way you're getting out of this jail. So, do you, or don't you?"

Rooster snorted. "I do—you know I do; I have to save Charlotte and Darla."

"By the power vested in me by the territorial governor of Nevada, I deputize you in the name of the law."

"Alright, you've had your fun," Rooster said. "Now, let me out of here."

He turned the key and let his friend out, but he was serious about making him his deputy.

"Let's get on the trail before the sun comes up and we lose the chance to surprise them."

Sheriff Tucker unlocked the rifles from the gun rack on the wall and handed two of them to Rooster and laid out two for himself. He grabbed a handful of ammunition from the box in his desk drawer, plucked out the tin badge next to it and tossed it to Rooster.

"Put that on; you'll need it."

Rooster pinned the tin star to his vest and the sheriff noticed the look in his eyes change.

"It's as if I just pinned on a little piece of my pa across my heart," he said.

The sheriff nodded. "Now you understand. That badge means something; wear it with honor."

Rooster smiled. "I will."

"Let's go get our wives back!" Sheriff Tucker said.

TWENTY

Charlotte and Darla worked quickly to tie the ends of the sheets together, so they could escape from the second-story window at Beau's ranch house. "We'll have to remove our dresses, or we'll never get down; they'll get caught on the trellis," Charlotte said.

Darla's hand flew to her mouth too late to conceal the loud gasp that escaped her lips. "I can't go traipsing through town in my bloomers!"

If she wasn't half scared to death right now, she'd have a good laugh at Darla's prim and proper, finishing-school attitude. "Darla, we're going to die or be married to Beau and his foreman if we don't get out of here—although I'm not sure which is worse, and all you're worried about is someone seeing you in your bloomers? I'd rather walk straight through the center of town in my bloomers alive than be buried in the most beautiful dress Beau's money can buy!"

Darla's lower lip quivered.

Charlotte sighed. "We can throw the dresses down to the ground and put them on when we get out of here, but we'll have to be quick," she said, tightening the last knot. "If Beau catches us before he returns from the mining camps, we won't be able to get away and warn our husbands about Beau's plan."

She tied one end of the linen *rope* to the leg of Beau's four-post bed and then hung it out the open window. From what she could see by the pale moonlight, the end was about six feet off he ground. They would have to jump the rest of the way.

"Are you ready?" Charlotte asked her shaking sister-in-law.

She nodded, but her quivering jaw and watery eyes showed hesitation. "I'm afraid," she admitted.

Charlotte hugged her. "I know you are, but I'll be right behind you."

"Behind me?"

Charlotte nodded. "I'm going to help you out first. No offense, Darla, but I don't trust that you'll climb down if I leave you behind to make that decision on your own."

She felt like a momma bird tossing her baby out of the nest, but now she knew why it was a necessary part of nature.

Darla began to whimper. "I can't do this; I'm not brave like you."

"Are you brave enough to put on the wedding dress Beau laid out on his bed for you and marry him?" Charlotte asked, clutching the woman's shoulders with a robust grip. "Because that's our future if we stay here. You heard what that man said; one of us better have that wedding dress on and be prepared to marry him when he gets back here. I don't know about you, but I'm not willing to sacrifice my new sister to that violent old man!"

Darla sniffled and wiped her face, jutting out her chin bravely. "Let's go before I lose my nerve!"

"Don't worry, this'll all be over before you know it," Charlotte said, walking over to the window with Darla.

"I'm afraid I'll fall," Darla said, turning back toward Charlotte, her limbs shaking.

Lord, don't make me have to push her.

"If you fall, a broken arm is a small price to pay, and better than spending the rest of your life with Beau!"

Darla drew in a long breath and blew it out with a whoosh. "You're right; I'll do this—for Rooster."

Charlotte smiled briefly. "Now you're talkin' like a true sister of mine!"

She dropped her dress out the window and watched it drift to the ground below, and then whipped her head around to face Charlotte, fresh tears welling up in her eyes.

"I can't do this!"

Charlotte put a hand under chin, forcing her to meet her gaze. "Yes, you can! Rooster taught me from the time I was little how to climb up and down from fruit trees that were taller than this house, using only a rope. We couldn't afford the fruit, and that was the only way we could get it. All you have to do is use the side of the house and that trellis to climb down; once your feet touch the house, all you do is walk down the side of it."

She nodded, but the fear remained in her eyes.

Charlotte showed her how to wrap the sheet around her wrist and helped her out of the window. She squealed when she dropped against the side of the house.

"Quiet, Darla," she warned. "We don't want to get caught. I've got you; get your balance and then shimmy down the side of the house the way I told you."

She watched Darla struggle and squeal.

"Be quiet," she whispered loudly out into the night air.

She let go of the breath she'd been holding in as soon as Darla landed on her feet on the ground. Then she tossed her dress out the window and tied a kerosene lantern to the end of the sheet and then lowered it to Darla.

She waited for Darla to untie the lantern and then gave the sheet a good tug before wrapping it around her wrist. She climbed out and lost her balance for a minute, a little squeal escaping her when she slammed into the trellis, but she immediately righted herself and made it to the ground safely.

"I guess it's been a while since I've climbed a tree," she said rubbing her backside. "None of them had thorns like the roses on the trellis; I feel like I've got a thorn in my caboose."

Charlotte wriggled into her dress and then turned around so Darla could fasten the top buttons and then did the same for her.

"I didn't think I was going to live through that, but it wasn't so bad," Darla said. "Where do we go from here?"

Charlotte looped the handle of the lit lantern over her arm. "To the mining camps to warn them Beau is going to blast; are you ready?"

Darla nodded.

"Hike up the bottom of your dress, Miss Darla, and let's run like we've got the Devil himself on the back of our heels!"

"Don't we?"

Darla hiked up her skirt and grabbed hold of Charlotte's hand and dragged her up to the road that led to the mining camps.

Who knew the girl could run that fast?

TWENTY~ONE

Rooster followed closely behind the sheriff, their horses running at full-speed. Suddenly, it was as if their horses had minds of their own; they snorted and squealed, and then locked their front legs and skidded on the trail nearly throwing Rooster and the sheriff from their mounts.

The ground rumbled beneath them, followed by an explosion.

The sheriff pointed toward the mining camps. "It came from that direction, but those miners wouldn't be blasting this time of night, and they know better than to use that much dynamite. They've probably caused a cave-in; let's go see."

Up ahead on the trail a lantern lit the way for two travelers. "Hey," Rooster said. "That's our wives!"

"Charlotte," Sheriff Tucker called out, leading the way. When he approached, he slid from his horse and pulled Charlotte into his arms, his emotions choking him. "I thought I was never going to see you again," he said, his voice shaky. "What're the you of two doing out here in the middle of the night?"

"We escaped from Beau's ranch," she said, with a shaky voice.

He could tell she was trying to control her emotions just as much as he was, and he loved her every bit for it. He tossed her up on his horse and mounted behind her. "Let's go, Deputy!" he said without looking back at Rooster.

"Deputy!" Charlotte and Darla said in unison.

Rooster pursed his lips and narrowed his brow, puffing out his chest just a little and jutting his chin. "I've been deputized; don't make a big deal of it."

Darla placed a hand over the tin star pinned over his heart and smiled. "It suits you, but you know that means you'll have to start wearing your gun."

"I think I can get used to that if you can," he said, helping her up onto his horse.

"Time's a wastin', Deputy!"

He climbed up behind Darla and set his horse at a fast trot, following closely behind the sheriff toward the mines.

Miners scrambled around lighting every lantern they could find to help them make their way in the dark. Worried conversations overlapped one another, and women-folk already gathered to build a fire to get strong coffee into the men who would likely be digging out the collapsed timbers well into the day. Charlotte and Darla filled their husbands in on Beau's plan to collapse the mine in order to strong-arm Rooster into reverting the mine back to him. He'd counted on Rooster giving up from frustration when he couldn't clean up the mess on his own and didn't have the means to pay workers to help him.

"Four men are trapped inside," Buford told the sheriff. "We can hear them about forty feet inside the entrance, but it's all collapsed between us and them."

"Do you know who they are?"

Buford nodded. "It's that snooty feller, Beau Dalton, who won the mine in a poker game. His men came out to talk to me yesterday when I struck a vein on my side of the rock, and now, tonight I overheard 'em say they were gonna use dynamite to blast, to see if there was more silver to be found."

"How many of the men are willing to help dig?" Rooster asked. "We've got to get them out of there."

"About thirty men, but a few of 'em are askin' why they should risk their lives for such an evil man and his men. They're the ones who caused the collapse."

"We've got to get them out of there because it's the right thing to do," the sheriff said. "But if the men don't want to help, I'm not going to order them to go in there. Me and my deputy will lead the search."

Buford's eyes widened. "You got yourself a deputy? Who'd ya git?"

Rooster stepped forward. "I'm the new deputy," he said, puffing out his chest a little to show off the tin star.

Buford flicked it with his finger. "Well, looky there; you got yourself a badge and everything! Ain't that gonna make Beau madder than a stampede of wild stallions?" the old man chuckled.

The three men went toward the opening of the collapsed mine to see what they could do to help. They stopped short, seeing the men carrying out the foreman from Beau's ranch. A thick layer of gray dust covered him from head to toe, and blood seeped from various scrapes. He held his arm close to his side, wincing every step. Doctor Goodwin would be needed to see to their needs, but for now, one of the women would tend his wounds.

"What about Beau and the other two men? Are they still alive?" the sheriff asked.

He coughed. "Milton and Cam are pretty close to the surface, but Beau is deeper in the mine. He wanted to collapse the entire mine so that Rooster couldn't work it and he'd come begging Beau to take it off his hands."

The foreman groaned trying to hold back a cough. He was in obvious pain.

"Why weren't you with the others?" Rooster asked.

He sighed. "I panicked; is that what you want to hear? I panicked and started to run out of the mine after the rumbling started, but I didn't make it out before the blast."

271

Rooster curled his lip in disgust. "I always knew you were a coward!"

"Rescue Milt and Cam, but leave Beau in there to rot the way he told us he was going to leave us in there!"

Rooster shook his head. "Sorry, ramrod, but we have to leave our personal feelings out of it. None of us has the right to decide when or how Beau Dalton dies. For now, I'm placing you under arrest for destruction of private property, reckless endangerment, and possibly murder, depending on how this all turns out at the end of the day."

Rooster handcuffed the foreman's good arm to the wagon tongue of the nearest buckboard. "If you're a prayin' man, now would be a good time to pray Beau makes it out of that mine in one piece or you'll be spending the rest of your days in the territorial prison."

The foreman hung his head.

Rooster rose from his haunches after he was satisfied his prisoner couldn't escape. "Let's go get that scoundrel out of my silver mine," he said.

The sheriff nodded, and they went into the mine, followed by the other miners. Rocks and timbers were endless as they began to dig their way to the trapped men. Minutes turned into hours before they came across Cam and Milt. By that time, the doc was on standby, and his services were needed with those two.

Sheriff Tucker wiped sweat from his brow, the grime from lifting and moving several hundred rocks throughout the day had left his aching limbs caked with multiple layers.

"I could use a bath," he said. "But I want to see this through. What do you think the chances are we'll find him alive?"

Rooster shook his head. "He's been too many hours in there with no air."

"We found him!" Buford said, leaning forward and bracing his hands on his knees to catch his breath.

Rooster and Sheriff Tucker walked toward him, but he raised his head and gave it a slow, mournful shake.

Rooster blew out a breath and motioned to the doctor and a few of the men. "Go in there and get him out," he said soberly. "We'll need a crew to take his body up to Boot Hill and bury him after the doc pronounces him."

Rooster stepped away from the others, the sheriff walking quietly next to him. He swiped his Stetson from his head and scrubbed at his ruddy hair, wiped the sweat from his brow with the back of his sleeve and then replaced his hat.

"Is this what it's like being a lawman?"

Sheriff Tucker nodded. "It gets pretty hectic at times, and then others, you get a nice long lull in the action and find yourself craving it."

"I don't think I'll ever crave a repeat of the last twenty-four-hours! The only thing I'll be craving is more time with my beautiful wife."

The sheriff caught Charlotte's gaze from across the camp and smiled. "I can get used to that kind of lull, myself."

Four men carried Beau's body from the wreckage and laid him on the ground in front of Doctor Goodwin.

The foreman watched as the doctor examined Beau for any signs of life, but didn't find any. He threw his head back and laughed.

Rooster kicked at his boot. "Have some respect, ramrod; your boss is dead, partly because of your carelessness."

He looked up at the sheriff. "I ain't laughin' b'cause he's dead; I'm laughing b'cause he left everything he owns to your wife, Darla!"

Sheriff Tucker and Charlotte bid goodbye to Deputy Rooster and Darla, who would be staying in town in the hotel until they could talk to Mr. Carter at the land office in the morning about buying the old Martin ranch.

It had been a long twenty-four hours, and everyone was ready for a good night of rest. So much had happened they were all a little overwhelmed and eager to get on with their future together.

The newlywed couple went inside the jailhouse, happy that the trying day was behind them.

"What happened to your hat?" Charlotte asked her husband.

"I had to rescue my hat from Millie Farmer's goat before I could rescue you," the sheriff said, regretting the words as soon as they escaped his lips.

"You rescued your hat before you came for me?"

"It's a long story, but it was necessary to get the hat back *first* or I wouldn't be here with you, now," he said.

She smiled and nudged him. "I'm guessing that's one of those stories that is really funny when you're telling it, but not so much when you're living it."

"It's kind of a funny story, but one that is better told after some time has gone by," he admitted. "But trust me when I tell you that if I hadn't rescued the hat first, I wouldn't have been able to come for you."

She bit her bottom lip. "When you do decide to tell me, remind me I've got a funny story to tell you, too!"

He suppressed a smile. "Does your story have anything to do with ladies' bloomers?"

She bit her bottom lip. "How did you know about that?"

"This is a small town and news travels fast."

She narrowed her eyes and tried her best to put on her angry-wife face. "Look here, Mr. Sheriff, if you already knew my story you shouldn't have agreed to let me hear yours later. It's not fair, and now I want to know why your hat needed to be rescued while your wife's life was in danger!"

He scooped her up in his arms and carried her into the oversized living quarters above the jailhouse. "Right now, I can think of something more fun than telling stories—Mrs. Sheriff!"

She giggled as he pressed his lips to hers.

Epilogue

One year later…

Rooster cleared his throat, a carving knife in one hand, a large fork in the other. "Before I cut into this turkey, I'd like to say a few words. First and foremost, I'd like to thank the one who cooked this bird, Henrietta Higgins, who most of us have known for too long as the Widow Colton, but I'm also thankful to Jasper, who finally got up enough nerve to marry her because I think they both deserve all the happiness in the world."

"I'd also like to thank Millie Farmer, for letting me have one of the smartest goats ever born—Little Millie. If not for her, some of us might still be locked in our own jail."

Laughter erupted among the guests.

"I'd also like to thank the sheriff, for marrying my sister and making her the happiest I've ever seen her, and for making me an uncle of the adorable little Clara—named after our ma, may she rest in peace. Most of all, I'd like to thank him for *tricking* me into being deputized."

More laughter.

"Seriously," he said. "Being a deputy has changed my life and so has marriage; I'm most thankful for my beautiful wife, Darla, and if she hadn't been another man's mail order bride, I wouldn't have had the courage to ask her to marry me, and we wouldn't have our beautiful newborn son, Harley—named after my pa, may he rest in peace. I hope he grows up to be a deputy just like the two generations before him.

This celebration dinner, as you all know is to honor our most *dishonorable* citizen for blowing up the Figg mine with dynamite and making me a silver miner. It ain't much compared to the Comstock Lode, but it's made us very comfortable, and we'd like to help by giving a little back to the community and helping with the church and the school. So, to Beau Dalton, may he rest in peace, for making so much possible for all of us here."

Sheriff Tucker cleared his throat. "The food is getting cold, Rooster; carve that bird so we can eat—or just pass it down to me. I'm so hungry I think I could eat the whole thing by myself."

"I agree with the sheriff; carve that bird, Mr. Fick!" the newly-married Henrietta said, winking at Darla.

Charlotte watched her brother carve the turkey, talking and laughing with their guests. He'd grown up so much—they both had.

Ma and Pa, if you're looking down from Heaven, I want to thank you for all you did for me on this earth. Now that I'm a new ma, it makes me appreciate all that you sacrificed and everything you went through to raise me and Rooster.

THE END

Coming Soon: Book 2

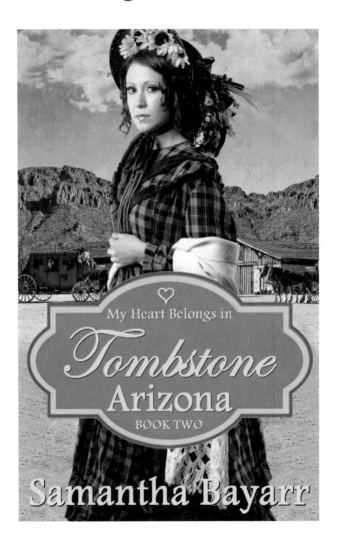

My Heart Belongs in Tombstone, Arizona

Beatrix Pruett is the new schoolmarm, but it doesn't take long for the women to put a committee together to revoke her invitation to the local sewing circle and to run her out of town.

Unable to figure out what she's done to offend them, she decides it's time to take action after she discovers she's been banned from church.

What's most confusing to her is why everyone in town keeps calling her Trixie.

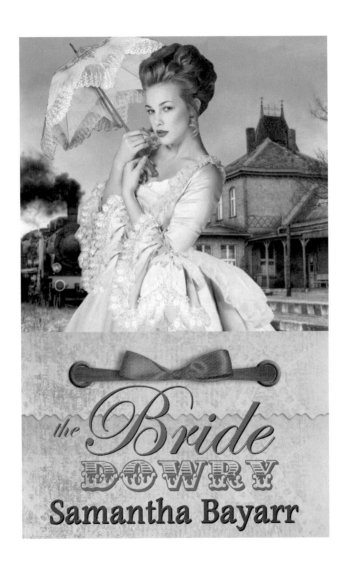

the *Bride*
DOWRY
Samantha Bayarr

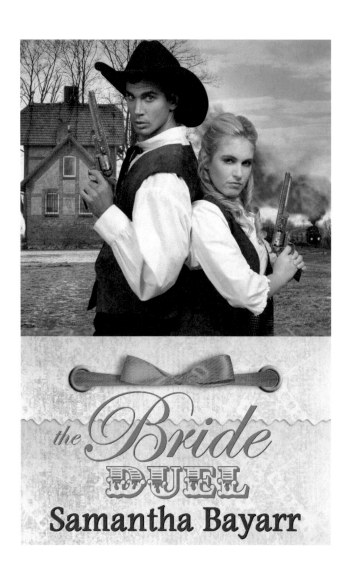

the *Bride*
DUEL

Samantha Bayarr

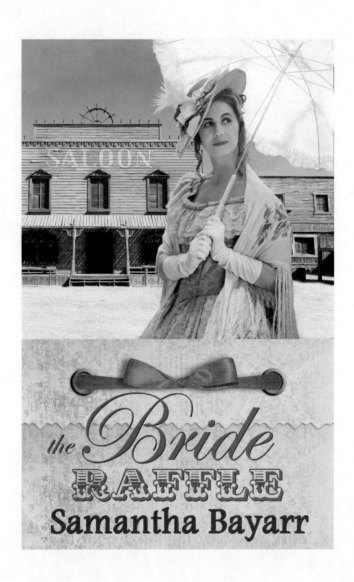

the *Bride*

RAFFLE

Samantha Bayarr

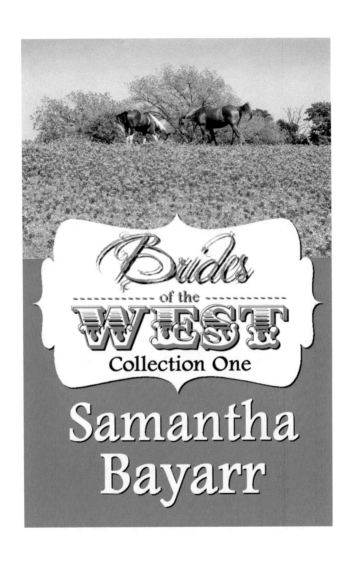

Brides
of the
WEST
Collection One

Samantha
Bayarr

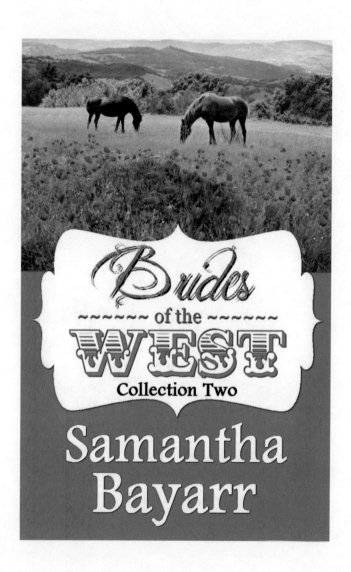

Brides
~~~~~~ of the ~~~~~~
WEST
Collection Two

Samantha
Bayarr

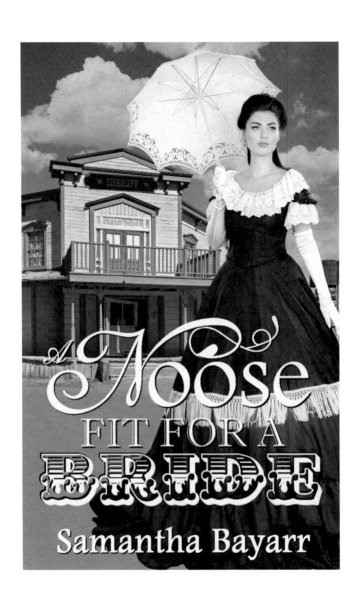

A Noose FIT FOR A BRIDE

Samantha Bayarr

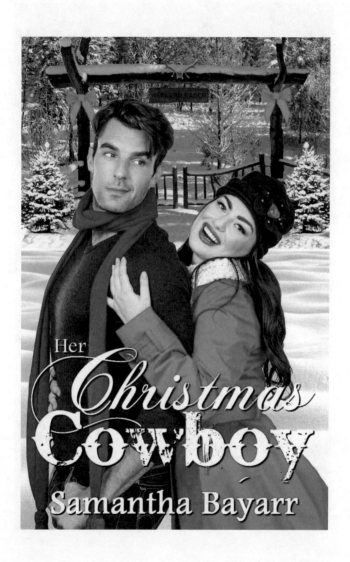

Her

Christmas

Cowboy

Samantha Bayarr

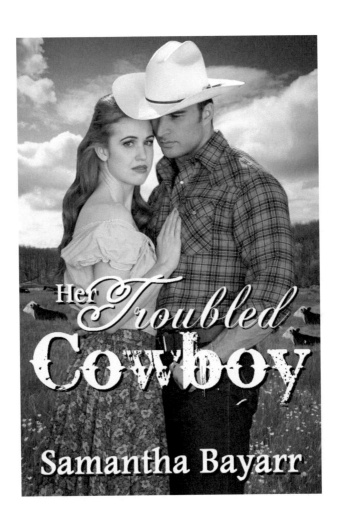

Her *Troubled* Cowboy

Samantha Bayarr

ABOUT THE AUTHOR

Samantha Bayarr, a former Paralegal, has written over 100 Christian Fiction Books in Contemporary Romance, Historical Romance, Western Romance, Amish Romance, and Amish Suspense.

She lives in an historical home in a small town in Florida with her husband, John Foster, who writes children's books. Samantha illustrates her husband's books, the first in the series entitled: Walla Walla and the Great Pirate Adventure. Check out these wonderful stories with a Christian message and over 50 full-color illustrations in each book.

Facebook LIKE HERE

 Follow me on Twitter HERE

Follow me on Pinterest HERE

 Follow my Blog HERE

Newly Released books
99 cents or FREE with
Kindle Unlimited.

♡ LOVE to Read?
♡ LOVE 99 cent Books?
♡ LOVE GIVEAWAYS?

SIGN UP NOW
Click the Link Below to Join
my Exclusive Mailing List

PLEASE CLICK <u>HERE</u> to SIGN UP!